"... walk.
Yo... tely."

Jacques pushed her back onto the soft sand, pinning her arms above her head with one hand. He covered her body with his, pressing close until she felt his skin warm against hers. Her lips reached to meet his, and Megan felt herself relax and respond to the demands of his kiss. When all the fight had gone out of her, Jacques kissed her eyelids, her cheeks, her throat, then he released her and relaxed beside her in the sand. Now she could feel the trembling of his body.

"And you say you don't care for me." Jacques touched Megan's cheek with his forefinger. "If there's anything I can't stand it's a liar."

ELLEN GOFORTH,
a woman of many talents, combines music, teaching and professional writing. She plays piano and trumpet and has published extensively for adults and children. The lush and exotic settings in her delightful romances are drawn from personal experience.

Dear Reader:

Silhouette Romances is an exciting new publishing venture. We will be presenting the very finest writers of contemporary romantic fiction as well as outstanding new talent in this field. It is our hope that our stories, our heroes and our heroines will give you, the reader, all you want from romantic fiction.

Also, *you* play an important part in our future plans for Silhouette Romances. We welcome any suggestions or comments on our books and I invite you to write to us at the address below.

So, enjoy this book and all the wonderful romances from Silhouette. They're for *you*!

Karen Solem
Editor-in-Chief
Silhouette Books
P.O. Box 769
New York, N.Y. 10019

ELLEN GOFORTH
Path of Desire

Silhouette *Romance*

Published by Silhouette Books New York

SILHOUETTE BOOKS, a Simon & Schuster Division of
GULF & WESTERN CORPORATION
1230 Avenue of the Americas, New York, N.Y. 10020

ISBN: 0-671-57005-6

First Silhouette printing May, 1980

10 9 8 7 6 5 4 3 2

Printed in the U.S.A.

Chapter One

Megan Taylor stood straight and held her head high when she smelled the scent of plumeria blossoms that wafted inside as her grandmother entered the apartment. Poise. That was one of the qualities she had tried to develop at business school. And now that poise must mask the insecurity she felt. Megan guessed her grandmother had never felt insecure in all her life. Gram might look like a froth of whipped cream, but underneath the fluff she was a bacon and beans type, dependable, steady.

Megan could hear Miss Rowe's business school voice do an instant replay in her mind. "Keep your demeanor strong," Miss Rowe had said. "Always appear to have a destination in mind and always appear to be heading directly toward it. Your enthusiasm will give you momentum. Remember—the world stands aside for those who know where they are going." Megan sighed. If only she knew for sure where she was going!

"Aren't you through packing yet, Megan?" Gram stepped briskly into the bedroom, peeled off her pink suit jacket, and stood for a moment under the overhead ceiling fan that stirred the heavy tropical air. "I was afraid you might have left before I got home."

Megan dropped onto the bed beside her open suitcase and smiled at her grandmother. Gram's hair was silver, but its pixie cut and her petite size-ten figure made her look much younger than her sixty years. Megan could set her watch by Gram's arrival home after her work day in the Canal Zone accounting office.

"I've just a few more shirts and scarves to tuck in, Gram." Megan stood again and added a rust-red scarf that matched her hair and an avocado-colored blouse to her suitcase. Miss Rowe had encouraged all her students to point up their assets, but Megan doubted that her red hair and green eyes would take her very far in the business world.

Determined not to let her grandmother suspect her inner qualms, Megan pumped bravado into her voice. "I don't know how I could be so lucky as to be chosen from all the girls in my graduating class to serve as secretary for the Yolanda Drive."

"You're efficient, that's why." Gram smiled and hung up her jacket. "And you'll make a good appearance, Megan. You've got a figure like a model—tall and willowy. Miss Rowe was looking for class as well as brains and business know-how when she chose you to work for Yolanda."

"Room. Board. Expenses. And that *fabulous* salary. Why, Gram, I'll be able to repay most of the money I owe you for business school tuition after just two weeks of working for Miss Delgado."

Gram patted Megan's cheek. "You owe me nothing, Megan. It was my privilege to help you."

Megan smiled. "Gram, years ago I used to envy other kids who had cookies-and-milk type grandmothers. Now I know how lucky I was to have a grandmother with a sense for business."

Gram slipped into a cotton eyelet robe. "I've always understood a woman's need to be able to make her own way in the world, Megan. That's why I suggested you enroll in business school for a more specialized education than the one your high school offered."

"And I owe you everything, Gram. Daddy meant well when he sent me to Aunt Lou's in Connecticut. I liked going to high school in the States, but I missed Panama. I'm glad you invited me back. A girl needs practical knowledge to succeed today. You gave me that when you paid my way to business school."

"It was the least I could do."

Megan shook her head. "I know you scrimped on essentials to meet my expenses. On my honor I'll repay you. And soon. You'll see."

Megan thought of all the things Gram could have bought with her tuition money. An air conditioner for the apartment. Taxi rides instead of standing room only rides on the crowded city buses. And Gram needed a nest egg to make her retirement years more secure.

Gram sighed and suddenly the wrinkles in her face stood out like lines on a relief map, pointing up her age. "Your father thought he was doing the right thing for you, Megan. He pictured you happily married to Vance, happily raising a family, and happily entertaining social and business acquaintances in some breeze-swept villa overlooking the sea. It was his dream for you."

Megan felt a lump block her throat as it did every time she thought of her father. Suicide. How miserable and frustrated he must have been to take his own life. How utterly unhappy. She knew how much his business had meant to him. He had poured all his money and energy into Taylor Tin after her mother had died ten years ago. But even his all had not been enough. The tin enterprise had floundered and failed. The two years since her father's death had aged Gram as well as herself.

"In one way you're lucky," Gram said. "I know you're thinking of your father's tragic death. But if Taylor Tin had remained solvent and productive you would have married a man who didn't love you. At least you were spared that. I don't know how Vance could have fooled us all so completely."

Megan sighed and nodded, knowing she would never fully recover from the wound Vance had etched on her heart. The minute Taylor Tin had declared bankruptcy and Vance had understood that he would never take it over as Chester Taylor's son-in-law, he had asked for his engagement ring back.

Megan felt her cheeks burning even now as she remembered the scene. Although she had wanted to stamp and scream and throw the diamond in Vance's face, she had held her emotions in check. She had laid the ring in Vance's hand calmly. She had kept her voice low. And she had walked from the room with grace and dignity. If the scene had been played on a stage surely she would have won a Tony.

Megan glanced at the false engagement ring she now wore on her third finger, a synthetic solitaire in a Tiffany setting of simulated gold. When the stone caught the light it flashed like the real thing.

"This ring is my protection against making the same mistake twice, Gram. No man is going to become interested in an engaged girl."

Gram snorted and tightened the sash on her robe with a yank. "You're running away, Megan. You're running and hiding behind a chunk of cheap costume jewelry. It'll never work."

Megan snapped her suitcase shut. "It will work. I'll see that it does. I want no more to do with men."

"You're a beautiful, talented girl, Megan." Gram stood back and studied Megan like a photographer about to take her picture. "Those emerald green eyes and that creamy complexion along with your rusty-red hair set off your willowy figure. Why try to fool yourself when it comes to men? Lie to me if you want. Lie to the world if you must. But at least be honest with yourself. The right man will come along one day and you'll forget all about Vance and the hurt he caused you."

Megan lugged her bag to the apartment door. Gram was right, of course. She was lying to herself. There was nothing in the world she wanted more than a husband whom she loved and who loved her in return, a home, a family. But she vowed to take a watchful, careful look at any man who tempted her to give her heart away again. She wouldn't be fooled by sweet talk under a tropic moon.

"Gram, my only regret about this job is that Jacques Ducruet is even remotely connected with it. I don't know why the Yolanda Drive headquarters have to be in his hotel. I'm not sure I can force myself to be civil to him should we meet."

Gram snapped on the overhead fan in the hallway and smiled encouragement. "It's unlikely that you'll meet Mr. Ducruet at all, Megan. I'm sure his personal life is far too full of the old cliché wine, women, and song for him to make any *personal* appearance at the Yolanda Drive headquarters. Jacques Ducruet is the type who lends his famous name to various enterprises, but seldom offers his actual presence. His brother, Michael, was like that too, but one seldom hears of Michael Ducruet these days. He seems to have dropped from sight."

Megan laughed in spite of herself. "Forewarned forearmed. That's my personal cliché. And I'll remember it, Gram. But if I should come in contact with Mr. Ducruet I know I shall have a hard time being civil."

"Mr. Ducruet really isn't at fault because he now owns Taylor Tin, Megan. Try to be fair about that fact. The Ducruet interests lie in the Ducruet warehouses in Colon's free zone. That's their big business. Taylor Tin went bankrupt. Down the tubes. Jacques Ducruet didn't cause that to happen."

"Maybe not. But he wasn't crying about it either."

"It was better for him to snap the business up, even though at a bargain price, than to have it dissolve into nothingness like salt in the sea."

"Right. I wouldn't have wanted that to happen."

"Your father gave his life as well as his fortune to that business. It's for the best that Taylor Tin continues even if it has to be under the Ducruet name."

"Of course. I'll try to remember that, should I meet Mr. Ducruet." Megan sighed. "I really can't admire Yolanda Delgado or anyone else who is such an out-and-out publicity seeker."

Gram nodded. "If you can't admire her at least try to respect her. Yolanda is trying to perform a community service. She's trying to raise a scholarship fund to provide educational opportunities for promising students from Panama City, from San Blas, from Taboga, and even from villages in the interior."

"I suspect that her motive in fronting the scholarship drive is strictly to promote Yolanda, Gram, but it's the end result that counts."

"Right. If even one young person benefits from an education received as a result of the Yolanda Drive, then the drive has been worthwhile."

"You've made your point. I know from experience how important an education can be."

Again Megan silently thanked her grandmother for sending her to business school, for enabling her to achieve competence in a field where she could work for financial independence.

Megan picked up the telephone. "Gram, I'm going to splurge and take a cab to Hotel Ducruet. Yolanda has promised to meet me there at six o'clock. I'll make a better first impression if I arrive by taxi rather than by bus. Anyway, I'd have trouble lugging this suitcase from the bus stop up the hill to the hotel."

"Of course," Gram said, then impulsively she added, "child, I'm going to miss you for these two weeks. Do call and report on how your job is going."

"I will. You know I will. And the job will go well. I'll see to that. In two weeks Yolanda Delgado will be writing me one of the best job recommendations I could hope for. Why, Gram, this job could be my springboard to becoming an executive secretary to some important company president."

Gram fanned herself with a newspaper. "Right. The Delgado name on a recommendation would carry a lot of clout."

After the farewells were said in the coolness of the apartment Megan stepped outside into the late afternoon heat and slid onto the sun-warmed taxi seat.

"Hotel Ducruet, please," she told the driver as she settled back to try to enjoy the ride from the Canal Zone through the posh residential districts of Panama to the section of the city where high-rise condominiums and Hotel Ducruet dominated a hill overlooking the sun-glinted waters of the harbor. January. True summer. It was a relief to know the rainy season was past for a few months.

The humid breeze wafting through the taxi window blew Megan's hair back from her face and cooled her cheeks. She could almost taste the sea salt in the air as she tried to concentrate on the palm-fringed avenues, the pink-blossomed oleanders that jeweled the medians, the scarlet hibiscus that bloomed with profusion in private gardens. But concentrating was impossible.

Ever since spending her high school years in Connecticut she had found it hard to accept the Panamanian taxi rides. Once she had jokingly told her father that everything in Panama moved at a mañana pace until one boarded a taxi. From that moment on it was a watch-out-here-I-come situation. Every driver operated his vehicle as if his fare had screamed "emergency" in his left ear and had slipped him an extra five dollars to hurry. This driver was no exception.

He honked at the car ahead of him as he prepared to pass it. He honked at the driver getting ready to turn onto the avenue. He honked and waved at a friend strolling on the sidewalk. Beep-beep. Beep-beep. Beep-beep. Megan found it impossible to close her ears to the din.

"Here are the ruins of the old city," the driver said, speaking to her over his shoulder as if she were a tourist. "Pirate Henry Morgan burned it over three hundred years ago."

"I know." Megan smiled at the driver who was watching her in the rear-view mirror. "I live here. I pass the Old City quite often."

The crumbling walls of cathedrals, shops, and other public buildings caught the fading rays of the late afternoon sun. Gray. Black. Bronze. Megan tried to count the different colors in the tumble of stones.

"The place makes you sad?" the driver asked, still watching her.

"In a way. How easy it is to destroy, but how difficult it is to create and build."

The driver shook his head as if he wasn't into philosophy.

Dark-skinned children laughed and shouted as they

played tag among the fallen stones of the ruined city. A gray and white kitten chased a ball into the tall grass at the base of a blackened foundation. For some reason when Megan tried to picture the long-ago Henry Morgan, a mental image of Jacques Ducruet flashed to her mind, dark hair and eyes, smiling eyes and lips set in sun-bronzed skin.

She had seen the Ducruet likeness often enough staring at her from the society pages of the *Star and Herald* or *La República*. Megan scowled. Maybe Jacques Ducruet was a sort of modern-day pirate. He frequently seemed to end up owning wealth that had once belonged to someone else.

The Ducruet name was well-known in Panama. Gram said it was because the family had come here from France years ago to help build the canal. But whatever the reason, everyone in Panama knew of the Ducruets.

"You have lived here always?" the cabbie asked.

Megan nodded. "My grandfather came to help build the canal."

"He was important man?"

She sighed and shook her head. "Today nobody remembers his name. He was just one of many workers who died of yellow fever during the years before the disease was conquered."

"Is sad," the driver said. "Those were hard days."

Deliberately Megan pulled her thoughts away from the cabbie, from the Ducruets, and from the Taylors and shifted them to Yolanda Delgado. She sat up straighter as she thought of the beautiful and sophisticated Yolanda, feeling frumpy by comparison. Typically Spanish in appearance, Yolanda flaunted her dark hair, always wearing it in a daring upsweep of combs and jewels. Yet she never let her hair detract from her

snapping eyes, her tanned skin, her voluptuous figure.
Megan had met Yolanda only once and that was at the
job interview. Of course she had seen pictures of her,
and always on the society pages of the newspapers.

YOLANDA DELGADO MODELS FOR HARPER'S
YOLANDA DELGADO VOTED PANAMA'S BEST-DRESSED
  WOMAN
  YOLANDA DELGADO HEADS THE YOLANDA DRIVE

"Here you are, miss," the taxi driver said, interrupt-
ing her thoughts as he drove up an incline and parked
near a sheltered portico that marked the hotel entry.

Megan sat for a moment drinking in the elegance of
the twenty-floor concrete hotel built in the shape of a
towering cylinder. Each room had its own balcony, and
many of these overlooked the harbor where a fleet of
shrimp boats had anchored for the night. Already
golden lights were flashing on in the hotel rooms.
Megan dug into her purse for the cab fare and a tip,
then she alighted from the car and followed the driver
through the tropical heat into the air-conditioned hotel
lobby where he set her bag down on the plush carpeting
beside the registration desk.

As Megan inhaled the fragrance from a bouquet of
plumeria the sudden change of temperatures brought
gooseflesh to her arms. She waited for a clerk to
confirm her reservation. She had never been inside
Hotel Ducruet before and she tried to study every
detail yet not appear to be awestruck should anyone be
watching her.

In the center of the lobby pastel-lighted fountains
splashed over three bronze dolphins who danced on
their tails in a rock-rimmed pool. Bamboo chairs
cushioned in dazzling tones of scarlet, gold, and blue

surrounded the fountain like jewels set in a ring. A wall hanging made of multi-colored bird and animal molas designed and appliqued by Indian women from the Cuna settlements in San Blas covered one whole wall area at the side of the registration desk. Megan recalled the $40 her father had splurged on a single mola blouse for her sixteenth birthday and she inwardly gasped at the probable worth of the unique wall hanging.

Across from the fountain five flagstone steps led down to a cocktail lounge and beyond that through an arched patio entrance Megan saw bikini-clad guests picking up towels and beach clogs from around the heart-shaped pool. Waiters were setting up poolside grills, and the scent of charcoal wafted into the lobby.

Palms and bamboo, philodendron and ivies formed a lush growth around what she could see of the poolside area, and she was about to step back for a broader view when a desk clerk spoke to her in Spanish. When she responded in English, he switched to that language with a smile.

"You have a reservation, miss?"

"I'm Megan Taylor. Yolanda Delgado is expecting me in the suite reserved for the Yolanda Drive."

"Ah yes, of course." The clerk consulted his reservation sheet, then he gave the black-uniformed bellboy a wrought-iron key and directed him to take Megan to the Delgado suite.

The noiseless elevator eased to a stop on the penthouse floor and the bellboy led the way down a green carpeted hall to a door padded in quilted velvet and marked DUCRUET SUITE. He gave a smart rap with the brass knocker and presently the door opened.

Megan looked up and up and up until her gaze met the dark, brooding eyes that had stared at her from the society pages so often. Inwardly she felt her stomach muscles tighten as she bristled with silent hostility. She knew without being told that she was face to face with Jacques Ducruet.

Chapter Two

Mixed with Megan's anger was the surprising thought that Jacques Ducruet's pictures failed to do him justice. They had failed to capture his overall football-hero look. She had never seen such an oh-I-want-to-touch suntan on any human. His skin had been toasted to a golden-brown hue and his face was enhanced by a perfect blade of a nose and eyes like deep-set obsidian. A cleft in his chin pointed up the sensuous curve of his mouth. When Megan realized she was staring she flushed and lowered her gaze. To her relief, the bellboy spoke and the softness of his unhurried voice helped her relax.

"Señorita Megan Taylor to see Señorita Yolanda Delgado."

Jacques Ducruet neither smiled nor seemed surprised. Casually he slid a tanned hand into the pocket of his white slacks, pulled out a bill and tipped the bellboy. "Señorita Taylor is expected. Gracias, Señor."

The bellboy turned, leaving them alone. In a moment Megan heard the whisper of the elevator door and she knew she was alone with Jacques Ducruet. She stiffened her spine and lifted her chin, forcing herself to meet this man with dignity if not with friendliness.

"There must be some mistake, sir." Megan made a

point of looking at her watch. "Miss Delgado was to meet me in her suite at six o'clock."

"There is no mistake." Jacques Ducruet smiled down at Megan with a sardonic gaze. "This is Miss Delgado's suite, at least it is hers for the time being. She has stepped out for a moment and has asked me to greet you, but she will return presently. Do step inside and make yourself comfortable."

Megan felt searing anger cramp her stomach muscles at the same time gooseflesh prickled her upper arms. She hated the thought of being alone with Jacques Ducruet. "But sir . . ."

"You needn't call me sir, Megan." Jacques used her first name as freely and as easily as if they were long-time friends. "I'm not your employer. Please call me Jacques. Yolanda speaks quite highly of you and I'm delighted to meet you."

Megan felt herself flushing as Jacques Ducruet devoured her with a practiced scrutiny, his gaze not missing any detail of her appearance as it roved from her face downward, lingering on her breasts, her hips, her legs, before it returned to meet her eyes.

His lips curled in a half smile. "Let me take your bag, Megan."

"Thank you."

Jacques Ducruet picked up her suitcase, motioned her inside the suite, then closed the door behind them.

Megan relaxed only a trifle as she looked at her surroundings. She had thought that Jacques Ducruet would be ushering her into a bedroom suite and she was pleasantly surprised to find that they were in a sitting room instead. A massive teakwood screen set in the center of the huge room divided it in half. The half Megan could see was furnished with palm-green, velvet-covered easy chairs, a teakwood table bearing wine decanters, crystal goblets and a silver service, and in a far corner, a large velvet-covered couch.

French impressionistic paintings decorated the walls, their bright hues bringing warmth and joy into the room. Somehow Megan felt that the Dutch masters with their dark, somber tones would have been more suitable for Jacques Ducruet—at least in his present mood.

Megan's heels sank into the plush carpeting, and she looked around the room until the silence between herself and her host made her squirm. For the first time she smelled the scent of roses and she stared at a single scarlet blossom in a crystal bowl on a coffee table.

"You like roses." Jacques made it a statement, not a question.

"I love them."

"The rose is my favorite flower too. You have excellent taste."

"What beautiful working quarters!" Megan exclaimed at last.

To her surprise Jacques laughed and eased like quicksilver into a contour chair. "What were you expecting, Megan? Pinebacked stools and a splintered council table? You should know that wouldn't be Yolanda's style. Or mine either for that matter. We both enjoy the good life."

Again Megan felt herself flushing like a child. How dare this man make fun of her! For a moment her business-school veneer cracked. She lost her poise and hurled her answer at him almost without thinking.

"As a matter of fact I was rather expecting an office atmosphere since Miss Delgado has hired me to do office work."

"Then I trust you're pleasantly surprised." Jacques splayed his tanned fingers on the chair arm in a way that suggested their great strength. "This palm-toned velvet

is a perfect foil for your auburn tresses and those green
cat eyes. Yolanda will be absolutely furious." Jacques
laughed half to himself as if the thought of Yolanda's
fury delighted him. Then he stared at Megan and his
gaze had a magnetic quality that held her captive
though she wanted to look away.

"Where is Miss Delgado?" Megan made no effort to
hide her growing hostility. "She said specifically that
she would meet me here at six." Somehow Megan
found the strength to break from the Ducruet gaze and
glance at her watch again. It was almost six thirty.

"You really didn't expect Yolanda to be on time now,
did you? Everything moves a bit slowly in the
tropics—especially Miss Delgado."

As Jacques rose and stood casually by the contour
chair Megan noticed the way his well-cut jacket draped
over his muscled shoulders, the way his silk slacks fit
like a second skin over his slim hips. Money. Everything about Jacques Ducruet seemed to shout of great
wealth. This man knew where he was going and the
world was standing aside for him.

While Megan noticed these things, he noticed that
she noticed and he gave her another sardonic smile.
She gritted her teeth to keep angry words in check.
How dare this man make her feel so self-conscious! She
smoothed her hair with her left hand, making sure he
saw her ring.

"If you're eager for someone to show you to your
private room I will be happy to do so." Jacques turned
slightly. "Come along with me, Megan."

Megan willed herself to show an outer calm while
inwardly she wondered how Jacques Ducruet could say
her name and make it sound like an endearment.
Darling. Sweetheart. Megan. His voice held a golden
resonance, a musical lilt like rosewood chimes echoing
across a moonlit sea. But why was she thinking such

things! This man was her sworn enemy, the enemy of what was left of the Taylor family. She hated the teasing look that danced in his eyes, teasing and testing as if daring her to succumb to his come-to-me glance, his provocative voice.

"Come along, I said." Jacques opened one of the three doors at the back of the sitting room and carried Megan's bag into a bedroom. As he brushed close to her the clean cool fragrance of lime surprised her. How had she expected Jacques Ducruet to smell? She blushed at her thoughts.

Jacques snapped on the light. The bedroom decor was in earthy tones—rust, beige, gray, muted green. A king-size bed dominated the room, the headboard forming a bookcase filled with leather-bound classics as well as with current best-sellers.

"You thought I was an illiterate clod?" Jacques followed Megan's surprised gaze.

"Th-this is your room?"

"It's my room when I'm in residence here." Jacques winked and grinned as if enjoying her discomfort. "It's not often that I let a strange woman, no matter how lovely, put me out of my own bed. Only for charity!"

"But I thought . . ." Megan stopped mid-sentence, reluctant to share her thoughts with this man.

"Just what did you think, Megan?" Jacques peered intently into her eyes. "You knew you were coming to a hotel suite. What did you expect?"

Megan walked across the room, slid open the glass doors, and stepped onto the balcony where she inhaled the sea air, warm, humid. In the last ebb of purple dusk she could make out the dark outlines of the shrimp fleet anchored in the harbor far below. Already the red, green, and yellow lights of the city were like bright specks of confetti decorating the hillside across the harbor. When she inhaled deeply she smelled the cloying scent of night-blooming jasmine. At last she stepped back into the bedroom and answered Jacques's question.

"Of course, Mr. Ducruet. I knew I was coming to a hotel suite."

"Jacques," he corrected.

Megan refused to use his given name. "I was under the impression that the suite which housed the charity headquarters belonged to Yolanda Delgado. That it was merely in your hotel."

Jacques shrugged. "That's exactly the impression Yolanda loves to give. But she didn't mislead you entirely. You needn't fear for your virtue. The suite is hers for the two weeks of the Yolanda Drive. It is she who will be in residence, and not I. You caught me here by surprise. I had just stopped by to pick up some business papers and Yolanda asked me to stay for a moment and greet you. I'll be going, so unpack now and make yourself at home. I insist."

Jacques reached for Megan's bag at the same time she reached for it and their fingers brushed for an instant.

"Excuse me." Megan jerked away as if she had touched a spiny sea urchin, and although she did not look at Jacques she could sense his suppressed laughter. And again she smelled the fresh lime scent that clung to his tanned skin.

"Relax, Megan. I don't bite."

Angry at her reactions to the embarrassing situation, Megan hesitated. Why was she behaving like an innocent schoolgirl! And why was Jacques Ducruet embarrassing her so! Why didn't he leave the premises? Surely he didn't expect her to unpack her things while he watched in fascination. Megan was mulling over what her next move would be when the door of the sitting room opened and Yolanda made her entrance.

Wearing a scarlet caftan that set off her dark hair and eyes and brushed lightly against her every curve, Yolanda swept across the sitting room like a prima donna searching for the spotlight. The heavy scent of gardenia traveled with her, reaching Megan an instant before she did. How old was this woman, Megan wondered. Then she wondered why she wondered. Whatever her age, Yolanda was in her prime.

"Oh, so you have arrived." Yolanda made no apology for her own tardiness.

"Yes, ma'am. Mr. Ducruet was kind enough to show me in." She nodded toward Jacques who had stepped into a dressing alcove that was hidden from Yolanda's view.

Yolanda's eyes widened only a bit at the sight of Jacques, but Megan noticed the not-so-subtle way Yolanda turned her voluptuous profile toward him.

"Yes, I am sure Mr. Ducruet was delighted to show you in." An ironic tone crept into Yolanda's voice. "Some say Mr. Ducruet is at his best when introducing a lady to a boudoir. Have you had dinner, Megan?"

"No . . . but . . ."

"No buts," Yolanda said. "Settle in. Unpack. Then call room service to send up your dinner. Whatever you want is yours—within reason." Yolanda glanced at Jacques before she uttered the last two words.

Jacques smiled at Megan, and his gaze never left her face as he spoke to Yolanda. "Perhaps Miss Taylor has a dinner engagement, Yolanda. Perhaps she prefers not to call room service. I doubt that such a lovely lady is used to dining alone."

Jacques looked pointedly at the ring on Megan's third finger, and Megan moved her hand from his sight, pretending to adjust the belt on her dress. She sensed that he was using flattery more to goad Yolanda into jealousy than to compliment her. But she didn't care.

She loathed his compliments, and surely Yolanda Delgado knew she had nothing to be jealous of. Megan only wanted Jacques Ducruet to leave.

"Miss Taylor has given up dating for the duration of this drive," Yolanda said to Jacques. "She is well paid for her self-denial, but I insist that she give her full attention to her work."

"Slave driver." Jacques grinned at Megan, but again his words were for Yolanda.

"When the drive gets into full swing it will be an around-the-clock situation." Yolanda closed her eyes, tilting her head in a way that made her dark lashes look like sooty wisps against her high cheekbones.

"Very well, Yolanda," Jacques said. "You're the bionic lady in charge of this drive. Far be it from me to tell you how to operate. But I do feel sorry for Miss Taylor's young man. If I were her suitor . . ."

"Out, Jacques." Yolanda said before he could finish his statement. "Miss Taylor and I have plans to discuss. Private plans."

Jacques shrugged. "I will call for you in an hour then. Right?"

Yolanda smiled up at him. "Right, Jacques. How could I forget?" Yolanda stood on tiptoe to brush a kiss on Jacques's cheek, but as she did so he winked at Megan then left without another word.

"Some hunk of man, isn't he?" Yolanda asked dreamily when the door closed behind Jacques.

"I really can't say since I've only met him this once." Megan was amused at Yolanda's possessiveness where Jacques Ducruet was concerned. Was it an affectation? Or was it spontaneous? Megan guessed that few things about Yolanda were unplanned.

"Some hunk of man," Yolanda repeated. "Take my word for it. In fact, that is an order. Take my word for everything where Jacques is concerned. But I need not tell you that, right? I have noticed the beautiful engagement ring you are wearing."

"Thank you." Silently Megan blessed Gram who had taught her that a simple thank you was all the reply necessary in response to any compliment.

"Megan, please go ahead and unpack your things. We will not start any real work until tomorrow. I just want you to settle in tonight, to relax, to get the feeling of these surroundings and relate them to a fund-raising situation."

"Thank you. I'll try."

"This is a special drive, you know." Yolanda paced, her caftan clinging to her ample curves. "This drive is aimed at Panama's wealthy. We are not begging coins from the common peasants on the street. The whole drive is to be geared to prying big money from a few of the wealthy who are quite willing to donate large sums if they receive status along with much posh entertainment. That is what they expect in return."

"I understand."

"There will be nothing of the office atmosphere showing to the patrons who visit this suite."

"I understand that too. But what kind of entertainment do you plan to provide?"

"I'll explain those details tomorrow. Right now I am wilted from a long session with a photographer and I must be ready to mesmerize Jacques in just one hour." Yolanda did a twirl in the center of the room. "Megan, if all my plans go well, I could be wearing Jacques's ring in two weeks from now. Mrs. Jacques Ducruet. How does that sound to you?"

Terrible, Megan thought. "Wonderful, Yolanda. Wonderful."

"Be a doll and help me unpack. Okay?"

Forgetting her own unpacked things Megan followed Yolanda to her room and tried not to be overly impressed when she saw mirrored walls reflecting a round bed covered in black satin and set in a floor of thick white carpeting. Boudoir chairs, tables, cushions—everything was decorated in black and white, and when Megan glanced overhead she saw that even the ceiling was mirrored.

"No comment?" Yolanda asked.

"Words fail me."

"Exactly the reaction my Jacques would enjoy. He loves to show off his guest room." Yolanda opened her scarlet suitcase. "Please hang up all my long gowns on hangers in the dressing room. I will take care of the other things."

Megan resented having to serve as Yolanda's personal maid, but she complied with the request, impressed with the chic Pucci and Dior originals she was handling. Silks. Satins. Sheer cottons. She had only seen such expensive gowns on the pages of *Vogue* and *Harper's Bazaar*. When she finished hanging the gowns she peeked into another large case.

"Shall I unpack this case, Miss Delgado?"

Yolanda flung open the case, revealing a stack of photographs of herself. "No, we'll not bother with these tonight. But first thing tomorrow the French stuff in the sitting room comes down and the Yolanda Delgado goes up. These pics are all from previous charity drives I have headed. They will be good advertising for this endeavor."

And good for Yolanda Delgado's ego, Megan thought sarcastically.

Once Yolanda's unpacking was finished, Megan retired to her own room. Behind her closed door she ordered a chilled seafood salad and half a papaya filled with orange sherbet. When the light supper arrived she ate it out on the balcony, enjoying the view of the harbor and, farther on, the city. The heady aroma of jasmine mingled with the sweet salt scent of the sea and Megan listened to the latin rhythms of a guitar, bass, and drum group playing somewhere nearby. Starlight Roof Garden? She had heard of that in connection with the hotel.

After dinner Megan left her balcony door open to admit the sea breeze as she settled down in bed with a slim volume of poems. How unusual, she thought. Jacques Ducruet did not seem the type who would enjoy poetry. Yet perhaps the mystical verses of Omar Khayyam rather suited him at that. She read one of the quatrains softly to herself:

> "And if the Wine you drink, the Lip you press,
> End in what All begins and ends in—yes;
> Think then you are TODAY what YESTER-
> DAY
> You were—Tomorrow you shall not be less.

Through her closed door Megan heard Yolanda and Jacques leave for dinner, then hours later when she was almost drowsing to sleep she heard them return. Yolanda's low laugh mingled with Jacques's sexy voice.

Megan covered her head with her pillow, but their voices coming from the next room wakened her fully. She stretched her warm body against the cool sheets and she couldn't help thinking that she was in a bed usually occupied by Jacques Ducruet. She was acutely conscious of her body resting perhaps in the very hollow where he had rested. She could almost see his tan against the muted green of the sheets. He had closed his mocking eyes; dark lashes shadowed his cheeks as he turned his head to place his curved mouth, warm and insistent, upon her own. Some hunk of man, Yolanda had said. Megan shivered and pulled the sheet protectingly under her chin. She lay awake for a long time listening to the low murmur of voices drifting from the next room.

Why should it bother her that Yolanda was entertaining Jacques? It certainly was none of her business. And she certainly had no interest in Jacques herself. Yet as she lay there in his bed with the tropical breeze wafting the scent of jasmine through the open doorway of her balcony she saw Jacques again in her mind's eye. She remembered the intimate way he had looked at her, his wink, the strength in his hands as he splayed his fingers against the velvet of the chair arm.

She could not deny that Jacques attracted her physically. But that was as far as she would allow the attraction to go. She and Jacques Ducruet had exactly nothing in common. She could think of no other man who could make her more miserable than he. She wondered if he even thought to associate her name with Taylor Tin which had so recently been changed to Ducruet Tin.

Chapter Three

The next morning Megan called room service and ordered guava juice, toast, and an anchovy omelette although she hated eating alone, especially in the confines of Jacques Ducruet's bedroom. The echo of his personality seemed to hover near and she found the sensation disturbing.

When her tray arrived jeweled with a sprig of

lavender bougainvillea, she carried it to the balcony and enjoyed a bird's-eye view of the city as well as the fragrance of the salt-scented air as she ate. The sound of early morning traffic whizzing by on Balboa Avenue far below was embellished by the cooing and chirping of doves that perched on the balcony rail waiting for a handout. Megan tossed a crust and watched as the doves quarreled over it.

Across the bottle-green water of the harbor the pristine spires of a cathedral spiked above the high-rise hotels near the banking district. In the other direction, on around the curve of Balboa Avenue, Megan watched gulls and pelicans wheeling above the yacht club where pleasure fishermen were preparing to go out for a day's fishing. In the distance cargo ships and oil tankers waited to enter the canal, and still farther out, the island of Taboga lay shrouded in the blue mist of early morning. Here in the fresh air and sunshine Megan's guava juice and omelette tasted better than she had thought they would and she lingered over breakfast until she heard the splash of Yolanda's shower. Moments later a knock sounded on her door.

"Yes?" Megan called.

"Am checking to see that you are up," Yolanda called back. "Soon we must start the business day."

"I'll be right out."

Megan carried her breakfast tray inside, showered, patted her lithe body dry, then stood before the clothing rod in the dressing room trying to decide what to wear. Idly she wondered how many times Jacques Ducruet had stood in this same spot wondering the same thing. She shivered slightly at the thought and wrapped a brown, velvet-cut towel around her nakedness.

Glancing into the mirror Megan smiled at her

reflection and thought of Gram who always claimed her granddaughter could wear a gunny sack and make it look like a party gown. But then, Gram was prejudiced. Still Megan was pleased with the way she looked. For a while Vance's jilting her had shaken her self-confidence, but earning her business school diploma had restored it somewhat. She had vowed to succeed as her own person. She didn't need Vance. She dressed, ran a comb through her shoulder-length hair, then opened the door and entered the sitting room. As if on signal Yolanda stepped from her room.

"*Buenos días*, Megan."

"Good morning, Yolanda." Suddenly Megan felt frumpy as she compared her own looks with those of the glamorous Yolanda. Megan inhaled the cloying sweetness of Yolanda's gardenia perfume and wished she had thought to touch a bit of scent to her own throat, her hairline. To reinforce the gardenia scent Yolanda wore a single gardenia blossom on a satin ribbon around her wrist. Megan wondered if Yolanda knew that Jacques preferred roses.

"Now nice you look this morning, Miss Delgado."

Yolanda preened before her reflection in a wall mirror. "You like my hair coiled into a crown effect?"

"Very much," Megan admitted.

Yolanda wore a flowing gown of saffron-colored silk that touched her ankles but which was slit up one side to reveal her shapely calf and thigh whenever she moved. Jet carved into star shapes dangled from her pierced ears, and she walked about the room on platform sandals with six-inch heels that accented her slim ankles and the curve of her calves. Megan sensed that Yolanda's awareness of her own looks made others aware of them also. Yolanda reminded her of a graceful panther about to pounce on its prey.

"Are you ready for me to begin work?" Megan marveled at the private feelings and thoughts her ordinary words masked. "Perhaps I should have dressed to match the velvet elegance of the sitting room. I do have a long gown with me."

"But no, Megan. You are my secretary. It is correct for you to appear in tailored attire suitable for taking dictation and typing letters." Yolanda scrutinized Megan and smiled. "Your French-cuffed blouse and jade-green skirt are perfect. And I always admire chunky gold necklaces and earrings. Yours compliment your gold bracelet."

Megan studied her bracelet with its single medallion struck in the shape of the entry gate at the old Taylor Tin factory. It was the last gift her father had given her and she cherished it almost beyond reason.

"Miss Delgado . . ." Megan began.

"Yolanda. Let's dispense with formalities. Please call me Yolanda and I'll call you Megan. Okay?"

Megan smiled and nodded although she sensed a certain falseness in Yolanda's friendliness. "Fine, Yolanda. Now if you'll tell me what my duties are, I'm ready to get busy."

Yolanda motioned for Megan to follow her to the area behind the teakwood screen. Here Megan saw a small desk, a typewriter, and a file cabinet. A green telephone on the desk matched the velvet couch and chair coverings.

"This will be your working area, Megan. As I told you I plan to keep the nuts and bolts of this fund drive from sight as much as possible."

"Of course," Megan murmured.

"Behind the screen you will write letters necessary for the drive. The initial brochure was mailed weeks ago. Now you will address envelopes in which you will

enclose supplementary flyers advertising the drive, and
you will keep account of all monies received in this
book." Yolanda pulled a blue account book from a
drawer and laid it on the desk top.

"What about money spent?" Megan asked, eager to
do things correctly. "Where is that account kept?"

Yolanda pulled a red account book from the desk
.drawer. "Money spent will be recorded in this book.
Money spent will come from my personal funds. All
money received will go directly into the scholarship
fund. I will pick up and pay all operating expenses."

Megan tried to overlook the bragging tone in
Yolanda's voice. "That is most generous of you,
Yolanda. I thought a charity's operating expenses were
always deducted from the money received."

Yolanda tilted her head and shrugged. "Yolanda
Delgado does things her own way. It is my unique
manner of donating to the Yolanda Drive."

Megan looked at the floor, avoiding Yolanda's gaze.
*It is your unique way of assuring yourself you will be
asked to head the fund drive*, she thought. *Your way of
buying yourself publicity that will attract male attention*.
Jacques Ducruet's attention? Surely Yolanda already
had that. Aloud Megan asked, "What do you wish for
me to do first, Miss Delgado . . . Yolanda?"

Yolanda laughed and the sound was like a low,
musical purr. "I told you that last night. Down come
the French Impressionists and up goes Yolanda
Delgado. You start taking down. I'll sta t putting up."

Megan nodded and did as she was ordered, removing
a Degas ballerina, a Cassatt madonna, and a Monet
from the sitting room wall and carrying them to her
quarters where she leaned them against the wall in the
dressing room. Returning for another group of paintings, she removed a Buffet, a Utrillo, a van Gogh.

Without the glowing pictures the room lost much of its elegance and spark, but Yolanda seemed not to notice . . . or to care.

Soon matted photos of Yolanda covered the walls. Yolanda shaking the President's hand. Yolanda presenting a check to the archbishop. Yolanda patting the head of a smiling orphan. Yolanda. Yolanda. Yolanda. Megan could barely comprehend such vanity. She watched the way Yolanda moved about the room, preening in front of each picture, adjusting it in minute detail, arranging table lamps so that each photograph was lighted to best advantage.

"Now you may distribute the scrapbooks," Yolanda said, seeing Megan standing idle.

"Scrapbooks?"

"In the suitcase in my room. They were packed under the photos. Bring them in and lay one on each table you see."

"What shall I do with the figurines that are on the tables?" Megan felt totally embarrassed by Yolanda's display of ego.

"Store them in your bottom desk drawer, Megan. It is empty and they will be safe there."

Reluctantly, Megan did as Yolanda requested, carefully wrapping Lalique crystal, English bone china, and Italian porcelains in tissue before confining them in the desk drawer. Jacques Ducruet had excellent taste. Megan glanced through one scrapbook and saw that it contained news clippings of Yolanda's activities in connection with other fund drives.

When all the pictures and the scrapbooks were in positions that pleased Yolanda, she turned to Megan. "Now you will make tea and coffee. Behind the screen, of course. Refreshments must be ready at all times. You will pour the brew into the silver service for serving our patrons. Most of them will prefer wine or perhaps a cocktail, but I want tea and coffee readily available."

Megan nodded. "I will see to it." She slipped behind the screen and hurried to a gleaming utility table she had noticed earlier. Filling a coffee pot and a tea pot with water and the proper ingredients, she plugged them in at the electric outlet.

"Oh, by the way, Megan. When a patron enters the suite you will stop any noise you might be making behind the screen. No typing, no telephoning—take the receiver off the hook. I will have symphonic music playing on the hi-fi for background. Get it?"

Megan was tempted to ask if it was all right for her to breathe, but she refrained. This was Yolanda's show; she would do as Yolanda ordered.

"Of course, Yolanda. But what if there are so many patrons in and out that I can't get all my work done?"

"Then you work after closing hours. We will have few patrons in and out until after the supplementary flyers are mailed. Seeing to the flyers is your first and most important work of the day. And remember, you are being paid well for your two weeks. Working after closing hours is a part of the package."

Megan flushed. "Of course." She said no more. She was beginning to like Yolanda less and less, but she could stand any work for two weeks, especially when the job meant so much to her. She was determined to please Yolanda even if she had to work around the clock. She planned to do everything in her power to get a good recommendation for whatever job she went to next. For a girl making her own way in the world, recommendations were important. And at the end of her two weeks Megan planned to repay Gram. That would be her big moment.

"I think the room looks perfect." Yolanda opened the scrapbook on the coffee table to a full-page photo of herself. Then she glanced around the room and nodded. "Yes, it is me. The whole room is Yolanda Delgado. Now do you have any questions before you start working on the flyers?"

Megan sighed, trying to decide which questions to ask first. Yolanda seemed to expect her to understand all about this operation. "First, I'd like to know what you're offering your patrons in exchange for their contributions. Yesterday you mentioned entertainment. But what sort of entertainment? Panama has much to offer."

Yolanda swept across the room and settled herself on the couch. "Bring your notepad and I will dictate material for the flyers. The brochure that went out weeks ago gave only a general picture of the entertainment to be offered. This supplementary flyer will give more specific information. It will tell what I plan to offer in exchange for contributions."

Megan hurried to her desk behind the screen, found a notepad in the center drawer and a ballpoint in a pen holder. Returning to Yolanda she started to sit down beside her, but Yolanda pointed to a straight chair nearby.

"Pull up a chair, Megan. It is more suitable for a secretary."

With flaming cheeks, Megan pulled the straight-backed chair near Yolanda and sat with pen poised.

"I will just give you generalities. You must embellish them with your professional business training. You must make them sound enticing to the wealthy patrons with whom we will be dealing."

"I'll do my best."

"The copy for the flyers must be completed by

mid-afternoon. The printer has promised me to have them ready by tomorrow morning."

"So soon?" Megan doubted that any Panamanian would or could act that swiftly.

"Of course. Money talks, Megan. And the more money, the louder its voice. The flyers will be ready by tomorrow morning. You can depend on that. You will address the envelopes today, stuff them tomorrow morning and have them in the mail before noon. In the meantime I will be making personal telephone calls to all the right people. The chosen. We will be dealing with a select few citizens, not with the huddled masses. The drive should be in full swing by day after tomorrow. People in my circle respond quickly when the cause is right."

Megan sat with pen and pad poised, wondering what it would be like to be one of the "select few" on Yolanda's list. Yet she had never considered herself a part of a huddled mass. "What will your first attraction be Yolanda?"

Yolanda smiled a self-satisfied smile as she answered. "Jacques has promised to fly patrons to Porvenier in his private plane for a day in the San Blas islands."

Megan could hardly believe she had heard correctly. Even she had visited San Blas. "But, haven't most of your . . . patrons seen San Blas before?"

"Odd as it may seem, most of them have not. The Cunas on San Blas have only recently opened their islands to the scrutiny of tourists. And that's mainly the type of people who have gone there—tourists from the United States, Mexico, Canada. Few of Panama's socially prominent residents have bothered to make the trip."

So she was a tourist. Megan smiled to herself. Maybe everyone was a tourist in his own special way. "Why do you think your patrons will bother to go to San Blas now?" Megan hoped Yolanda wouldn't think her question impertinent.

"Bother?" Yolanda raised her eyebrows and her bosom heaved as she inhaled deeply. "Now my patrons will vie for the chance to fly to San Blas. I will make it seem the thing to do. People will sign up for the flight because the Delgado name and the Ducruet name will make visiting San Blas an *in* thing to do. I use psychology, Megan."

"Can you give me some suggestions for wording the flyer?"

"People will love to be able to say they have flown in Jacques Ducruet's private plane. Make that your first point. No . . . wait . . . put this first. They will love to brag that they have eaten lobster salad made from Yolanda Delgado's famous recipe, that they have sipped vintage wine with Yolanda Delgado on the breeze-swept veranda of Porvenier's only hotel. I have rented the islands for the day, Megan. No ordinary tourists will be allowed on the San Blas islands that day—just patrons of the Yolanda Drive. You will know the right words to use in presenting this tour in the flyer."

"How much space will I have?" Megan wondered if she really would find the right words. Yolanda said everything twice for emphasis, but a writer couldn't do that.

Yolanda thought for a moment. "Perhaps 200 words for each event. That should leave enough space to list the names of last year's patrons and the amounts of their contributions. Such a listing tends to keep contributions high. Nobody likes to lose face."

Megan thought she had never heard of such snobbishness, but she kept her voice pleasant. "And what is the next event? And the date?"

Yolanda thought for a moment before replying. "On this coming weekend Jacques has agreed to take a select group of people deep-sea fishing on his private yacht. Of course, this event may appeal more to men than to ladies but . . ."

"And where will they fish?" Megan wrote down all the details she could pry from Yolanda.

"I wanted Jacques to take the patrons down Colombia way," Yolanda said. "But he says that is too far and too impractical for a single day's outing. So he will take them to the waters near Contadora. Mention in the blurb that they may catch billfish and marlin of trophy size."

Megan jotted down the facts, wondering all the while why Jacques Ducruet was being so generous and thinking that perhaps the fund raising should have been called the Ducruet Drive. The name certainly would have been more alliterative. She said nothing. It was not her place to criticise. But she wondered if Yolanda was trying to impress Jacques or if Jacques was trying to impress Yolanda. No matter. They would be giving the money to a good cause.

Yolanda poured herself a cup of coffee but she did not offer Megan one. She settled herself on the couch once more and continued dictating.

"Another event to take place the first of the second week of my drive will be a moonlight launch ride to Taboga where a calypso group will provide music for dancing under the tropical stars. I plan to rent the Taboga hotel and its beach for this event. A midnight supper will be served, and later an early-morning breakfast."

"Sounds fantastic," Megan said, truthfully. "I've lived in Panama most of my life, but I've never been to Taboga. I've always meant to go over sometime, but I just never got around to it. Whenever we took a vacation or a day off Daddy always preferred the beaches at Contadora."

"I agree with his good taste completely," Yolanda said smugly. "And as a climax to the two-week drive, Jacques has agreed to open his villa on Contadora for a gala party. Dinner and dancing."

"He owns a home over there too?"

Yolanda shrugged. "Why not? He can hardly entertain a large group in this penthouse suite, and his home in Colón is very secluded and private. His main business is operating warehouses in the Free Zone. He entertains manufacturers and shipping magnates from all over the world, and the villa on Contadora is the one he uses for such parties."

Just then someone rapped on the door. Megan jumped, startled, but Yolanda rose slowly, smoothed the saffron silk of her gown over her hips and moistened her lips with the tip of her tongue.

"Behind the screen, Megan, if you don't mind. Check the coffee pot and the tea service. Have them in readiness. Then you may begin work on the flyer, but do your rough draft in longhand. No typing until our guest leaves." Yolanda turned the hi-fi volume up a bit and glided toward the door.

Chapter Four

Feeling like a ragamuffin who must be hidden from company, Megan slipped to her station behind the teakwood screen. She knew she should begin writing copy for the flyer if she was to have it to the printer on time, but her curiosity got the best of her and she listened to the conversation taking place on the other side of the screen.

"Señora Alveriz!" Yolanda exclaimed. "How nice of you to take time to stop by. I was hoping you would lend your support to my charity."

"I'm so glad you telephoned me, Yolanda." Señora Alveriz's voice was throaty and low, and as Megan listened she tried to guess what the lady must look like. Then suddenly she had to guess no longer. She found a pea-sized hole in the carving on the teakwood screen and she peeked through it at the caller.

Señora Alveriz was small but well built. She wore a pantsuit of avocado green silk and her butter-blond hair hung in a pageboy fall reaching to her narrow shoulders. Was it a wig? Her carefully manicured hands lay quietly in her lap and the jeweled rings on her slim fingers glinted as the lamplight struck them.

"I do want to participate in one of the events you are offering," Señora Alveriz said, "but I have no desire to visit the Indians on San Blas, and I gave up fishing long ago."

"Perhaps you'd enjoy the moonlight launch ride," Yolanda suggested.

Megan saw Señora Alveriz shake her head. "No. Since my husband passed away I care no more for dancing under the stars. But I do believe I'll attend the gala on Contadora. I've always wanted to see Jacques Ducruet's villa over there. I've heard fantastic things about it . . . about his lifestyle."

Yolanda served Señora Alveriz a cup of tea and smiled down at her. "I'm sure all you've heard about the Ducruet villa is true. The gala there is to be one of the prime attractions of the drive. And of course Jacques has promised me to be there in person and to chat with all the ladies."

Señora Alveriz set her tea cup aside and pulled her checkbook from her shoulder bag. "Would a thousand dollars be acceptable, Yolanda?"

Megan stifled a gasp and watched the way Yolanda kept her cool, smiling, but never showing any excitement. "Why, of course, Señora Alveriz. A thousand dollars would be adequate."

Adequate! Megan couldn't believe her ears. *Adequate*! What did Yolanda expect in the way of donations? What would she consider grand? Megan was still mulling over the question in her mind when Señora Alveriz left the suite and Yolanda called out to her.

"You can use the typewriter now, Megan. She's gone. And she has left me a thou! I caught a big one on my first try."

Megan sighed. So Yolanda *was* impressed with the thousand-dollar gift after all!

Megan had just started typing rough draft material for the flyer when the door to the suite burst open and someone entered without knocking. Megan stopped the typewriter noise immediately.

"Jacques!" Yolanda exclaimed in mock dismay. "I really expect people to knock before entering."

Megan peered through the peephole at Jacques, irritated to notice that the mere sight of the man set her heart to beating more rapidly than usual. And why was her mouth so dry! Today a white shirt and sea-blue slacks set off his golden tan, and Megan could see his shoulder muscles ripple beneath the thin silky fabric. She had a sudden desire to smooth the fabric with her fingers, to feel the way it clung to his skin.

"I'm unaccustomed to knocking on my own doors," Jacques said, "but I'll try to remember to do so in the future if it will please you."

Jacques's deep-throated voice drew Megan like a magnet and again she watched through the peephole as Yolanda sidled up to him, linked her arm through his, and gazed up into his eyes. Megan imagined the way Jacques's warm skin must feel against Yolanda's arm, and although she wanted to look away, she couldn't take her eyes off Jacques.

"Of course I shouldn't have expected *you* to knock, Jacques." Yolanda led him to the sofa and sat down, pulling him down beside her. "What is on your mind this morning, darling, besides me, of course?" Yolanda cupped her hand over Jacques's knee, her forearm resting lightly along the length of his thigh.

Jacques eased a few inches from Yolanda. "I'm afraid I'm going to have to back out on my offer of letting you use the complete suite, Yolanda. At least for this afternoon. I need my private room for a . . . conference."

Megan could see Jacques look toward the third door at the back of the sitting room, but she couldn't see Yolanda's expression. She felt herself tense as she realized Jacques was going to be close by, at least for part of the day.

"But of course, Jacques," Yolanda said. "The room

is yours, is it not?" She tweaked him playfully on the ear and he edged a bit farther away from her.

"It is, of course," Jacques agreed. "I just want to make sure you know I have a conference and I want it understood that I do not want to be disturbed."

"I can arrange for perfect privacy—for a price." Yolanda tilted her head and looked up at him provocatively.

"A price?"

"But of course. These are my headquarters for a charity drive. You can prove to me that I am your favorite charity by taking me to the Panamar for lunch. Is that too great a price to pay for an afternoon's privacy? We'll have a glass of wine, a salad and an intimate conversation."

Megan stopped watching the scene playing on the other side of the screen and she wished she could turn her ears off as well. It was no concern of hers who Jacques Ducruet took to lunch. Yet she kept listening in spite of herself. What if Jacques had other plans for lunch? What if he didn't care for an intimate conversation with Yolanda? Yolanda was not the sort of person who accepted no for an answer.

"You may call for me a little before noon," Yolanda said, "and I will instruct my secretary to admit you to your private quarters this afternoon while I am out at the hairdresser's. Is that fair?"

"Your secretary—Miss Taylor?" Jacques laughed, his eyes crinkling at the corners. "How are you and the little spitfire getting along so far?"

"Little spitfire?" Yolanda peered at Jacques through narrowed lids. "Miss Taylor seems rather mousey to me."

"I wouldn't be too sure." Jacques grinned. "I think she's a girl who'll speak her mind if given half a chance. You just may have met your match, Yolanda."

Megan felt herself flushing even though neither Yolanda nor Jacques could see her. Surely Jacques knew she was behind the screen. Surely he was trying to goad her into an angry outburst that would infuriate Yolanda. Her hands balled into fists. Well, she wouldn't let that happen. Poise. Poise. Not for anything in this world would she let Jacques cause her to jeopardize her job. These two weeks meant too much to her to let anyone spoil them. Megan pressed her lips into a thin line and vowed to keep silent no matter what happened on the other side of the screen, no matter what Jacques said or did.

But in spite of herself she watched through the peephole again. Jacques started to rise from the couch, but Yolanda laid a smooth, well-manicured hand on his arm.

"Surely you can stay long enough to have a cup of tea with me, Jacques. One moment and I will serve it to you."

Jacques sighed and settled back onto the couch. "Make it coffee, Yolanda. Black. And strong. You know I hate tea. I always think of it as an old lady's drink."

Megan rose, ready to pour the coffee for Yolanda, but when Yolanda stepped behind the screen, she motioned Megan aside and poured the coffee herself. She poured a second cup, adding sugar and cream, then she carried the two drinks to the other side of the screen like a queen carrying the crown jewels to the king.

By the time Yolanda returned with the coffee, Jacques had left the couch. Megan could see his handsome profile as he studied the photographs on the walls.

"I see you have made the room yours in your own

inimitable way." Sarcasm crept into his tone as he scowled at Yolanda.

"The patrons like to see my picture. They like to know they are associating with *the* Yolanda Delgado, darling of photographers and TV interviewers. I only wish you were as impressed as most of my public."

Yolanda offered the cup of coffee to Jacques just as he turned swiftly from one of her pictures. His elbow caught the cup, dashing the scalding liquid onto his arm and leg. A brown stain spread on his blue slacks and a puddle of coffee oozed into the carpet.

As the coffee scalded Jacques, he flinched, accidentally bumping into the teakwood screen and toppling it over onto Megan who cried out in pain and surprise. The wooden fram hit her arm, pinching it against the desk. For a moment the stabbing pain in her wrist and the sharp smell of the coffee made her feel faint and dizzy.

"Jacques!" Yolanda exclaimed. "You poor, poor thing. Let me get some ice for your burns."

Jacques recovered his composure in an instant and rushed to lift the screen.

"Megan . . . Miss Taylor!" he shouted. "Are you all right?" He dashed around the screen and knelt at her side.

He remembered my name. Megan shook her head to clear it, ignoring the pain in her arm and hand. He remembered my name. Then she bristled with hostility toward Jacques as well as with anger at herself for her crazy thoughts. How could she think of Jacques Ducruet when her wrist might be broken? Yolanda Delgado would have no use for a secretary with a broken wrist!

"I say, are you all right?" Jacques took Megan's hand gently in his own. "I had no idea anyone else was in the room. I apologize for my clumsiness. Do answer me, Megan. Are you all right?"

Megan felt as if she were in shock. Outwardly she scowled at this man who aroused such hostility in her, yet, at the same time her heart pounded in response to his nearness to the fresh-lime fragrance of his skin, to the strong, capable hand now gripping hers. She had no desire to pull away her hand, no will to say the words that would end his concern for her. But she must find the strength to pretend. . . . No, it would not be pretending. There was no need to pretend. She had good reason to hate this man who had aroused her senses against her will.

"Megan, answer me." Now Jacques towered before her but Megan was distracted as her gaze fell on her wrist. The screen had scratched her arm and at the same time it had torn her bracelet off and snapped the medallion from it. Oblivious to her injured arm, Megan glared at Jacques, seeing him through the red haze of her anger.

First you take Taylor Tin from us, she thought, *and now you damage my last remaining token of the family business my father gave his very life to*. All poise and grace left her as she lashed out at Jacques Ducruet, trying to hurt him as much as he had hurt her.

"You are a clumsy oaf, Mr. Jacques Ducruet." Megan heard her voice deadly and cold. "Has anyone dared tell you that truth before?"

"My heartfelt apologies, Megan. I'll call my personal doctor to tend to your arm."

Megan stepped back, trying to avoid Jacques's hands as he reached toward her again. But she was too late. Jacques Ducruet held her hand in his powerful grip as he examined the scratch on her arm and her wrist. Megan felt her pulse throb in her hand, knowing that

Jacques must feel it also. With eyes blazing she jerked her hand free from his grasp. She imagined she could feel the warm imprint of his fingers on her skin. Clearly, her wrist was not broken.

"I don't want your doctor, Mr. Ducruet. My arm will heal. The scratch is minor. But you have destroyed a bracelet that had much sentimental value to me."

"Bracelets can be replaced, Megan." Yolanda spoke for the first time since the accident. "Surely you will not have the audacity to trouble Mr. Ducruet over a silly piece of costume jewelry. I will replace it for you myself, replace it with something of value from my own jewelry collection. Think no more of this, Jacques. The girl is hysterical. Be on your way and I will calm her after you leave."

Ignoring Yolanda, Jacques stooped to pick up the bracelet and the medallion. Megan snatched at the glinting metal, but Jacques held it out of her reach, examining it carefully. Then he looked at her, the full impact of his gaze meeting the full impact of hers.

"Taylor Tin? Why are you wearing such a strange medallion?"

"As if you care! My own father's business belongs to you now. Taylor Tin no longer exists. You've destroyed the Taylor name and replaced it with your own. And now you've also destroyed the only remembrance I had of the business my father devoted his entire life to."

Megan was surprised to see Jacques's expression suddenly soften. His mouth relaxed and the pupils of his eyes grew large and black.

"Megan *Taylor*. So that's who you are. Megan Taylor of Taylor Tin."

"A lot you care!"

"I might care more if you weren't such a spitfire." Now Jacques's eyes blazed and he backed off, brushing into Yolanda who stood at his elbow watching the scene with surprise and indignation.

Spitfire. Something in the word and the way Jacques said it made Megan want to yank back her angry words, but it was far too late for that. Where was her poise? She knew she should make amends, yet somehow she couldn't bring herself to apologize to Jacques Ducruet. Using all the dignity she could muster, she turned and retreated to her room, quietly closing the door behind herself when every instinct made her want to give it a resounding slam.

It was some moments before Yolanda knocked softly then entered without invitation. "If you have composed yourself, I want a word with you."

"Of course." Megan looked at the floor, hoping Yolanda wasn't going to fire her on the spot. "I'll apologize to Mr. Ducruet if you wish. I was shamefully outspoken."

"No apology is necessary. But I hope you have learned a lesson."

"A lesson?" Megan felt her temper threaten to flare again. She certainly had learned nothing from Jacques Ducruet that she hadn't already known.

"The lesson is to avoid Jacques. He is dangerous man. He can be quite savage when aroused."

Megan felt anger boiling inside her. "You needn't tell me that. I don't plan to have anything to do with him."

Yolanda looked at her in an infuriating manner. "Do not lie to yourself, Megan. I saw the looks that passed between you and Jacques. I know you are attracted to him. I am not surprised. All women are attracted to Jacques. And do not for one little moment think he does not make the most of his advantage."

"I certainly am not attracted to Mr. Ducruet."

"Forget him, Megan. You have no chance with him.

Jacques Ducruet can have any woman in Panama that he desires. Don't you realize that? He is not apt to want a little secretary fresh from business school. Furthermore, I cannot afford to have your mind distracted from the details of the Yolanda Drive. Please forget Jacques Ducruet. That is an order."

Megan wanted to lash out at Yolanda, wanted to pack her bag and leave immediately, but now her manners came to her aid in the moment of decision. Yolanda was right. She was a mere secretary and as a mere secretary she needed this job. She couldn't afford to let her sharp tongue cost her this position. She would find the poise and wisdom necessary for dealing with Jacques and with Yolanda.

Megan forced a smile. "You are right, Yolanda. Give me five minutes to bathe my face and I'll be ready to devote my entire attention to the Yolanda Drive."

Chapter Five

Megan bathed her face in cool water, applied fresh makeup, then returned to her desk and her duties. Although she presented a calm front to Yolanda, the knowledge that Jacques Ducruet had the power to arouse such a tempestuous reaction in her frightened her. She vowed to keep her guard up against him in the future.

One other patron arrived that morning in response to Yolanda's telephone campaign, and for the most part the hours passed quietly. Megan continued her typing when Jacques arrived to take Yolanda to the Panamar and only after they had left the suite did she order an avocado salad and minted tea sent up to the suite. Idly she wondered what it would be like to lunch with Jacques Ducruet. Did he cup his strong hand under a lady's elbow as he guided her to a table? Did he order for a lady or did he let her choose her own fare? Did his luncheons end promptly or did they extend into the siesta hour with more wine and soft music and perhaps a darkened room? Megan sighed. Clearly, Yolanda had planned another kind of an afternoon for her lowly secretary.

Leaving the door to her room open, Megan carried her lunch to her private balcony, knowing she would be able to hear any knock on the door should another patron arrive. But nobody came. Megan watched gulls and pelicans wheel and dive against the backdrop of a cloud-fluffed Panamanian sky as she ate. How was she going to tolerate two weeks of solitary dining?

"I'll keep my mind on my work and I will not complain," Megan said to a dove perched on her balcony rail. "So I'm talking to the birds! This job is my stepping stone to great things. Once the plane flights and the yacht trips begin I'll be busy day and night. I'm going to relax and enjoy these first days of relative ease."

The dove cocked its head, then flew down to the pool area. Megan had just set her meal tray aside when Yolanda returned. It bothered her to realize that she was glad Yolanda and Jacques hadn't lunched through siesta. Jacques was not with Yolanda and Megan breathed a sigh of relief at being spared more of his company.

"Buenas tardes," Megan called to Yolanda for the sake of being polite to her boss. "Did you have a pleasant lunch?"

"The Panamar was absolutely wonderful as usual,"

Yolanda said, beaming. "Simply wonderful. Estéban, the head waiter, saved us a seaside table. I've never seen so many ships in the harbor. And sailboats too. Of course the broiled lobster was delicious as always, and only Jacques himself could toss a better salad."

"Jacques cooks?" Megan was surprised that Jacques Ducruet would be interested in such an occupation.

"But of course Jacques cooks. Jacques fancies himself quite a chef. He often prepares dinner for the two of us at his secluded home in Colón. French-fried plantain. Crêpes. Steak. But of course you wouldn't know about that."

Megan squelched the flame of anger that spurted in response to Yolanda's put-down. And she felt a twinge of envy as she thought of Yolanda and Jacques sharing an intimate dinner for two—a dinner which Jacques had prepared. But how foolish! She had no romantic interest in Jacques Ducruet. He was the type who could only make her miserable. Circumstances beyond her control had made them enemies, and even if there had been a friendly platonic relationship between them she would not allow herself to be romantically interested in Jacques or in any other man. She adjusted the solitaire on her third finger and resumed her typing on the rough draft of the flyer.

"I'll be away most of the afternoon," Yolanda said. "In case of an emergency you can reach me at Henri's Salon just off Via España. However, I foresee no emergencies." Yolanda went to her room to freshen her makeup and when she finished she paused at Megan's desk, wafting the scent of gardenia with her every movement.

"You understand about listing the patrons' names?" Yolanda asked.

"I have the sheet of figures right here."

"Good. The task is merely one of copying the correct data."

As she glanced at the sheet Megan marveled at the list of names. "Panama is such a cosmopolitan city, isn't it? Lefevre. Mendez. Sullivan. Iglesias. French. Spanish. Irish. Indian."

"The names reflect the nationalities of the people who settled in Panama years ago," Yolanda said. "Many of them came to work on the canal or to cater to others who were working on the canal. Some people had made fortunes in Panama, others, while not so wealthy, found a pleasant and rewarding way of life in this country of perpetual summer." Yolanda laid her hand on Megan's shoulder.

"You have more instructions?" Megan looked up at her, notebook in hand.

"Jacques is in his private quarters now and he is not to be disturbed. I do hope that is clearly understood."

"But how did he . . ."

"He has a private entry, of course. Just see that nobody disturbs him from this part of the suite. Do you understand?"

Megan flushed as she nodded. Did Yolanda think she was going to go knocking on Jacques's door the minute she was out of sight!

"Of course, Yolanda. Jacques will not be disturbed by anyone in this room. As far as I am concerned Mr. Ducruet is not in residence here at all."

"That's good." Yolanda picked up her purse. "I will be on my way now, leaving you in charge. Please have the flyer copy ready for my inspection when I return shortly after three o'clock. That will give me time to get it to the printer before he closes."

"I'll have it ready, Yolanda."

Yolanda left the suite and Megan had typed no more

than a few paragraphs when Jacques stood framed in the open doorway of his private room. He had changed from the coffee-stained slacks into a one-piece leisure suit the color of ripe limes. In one tanned hand he carried some L-shaped pine braces and in the other hand he held hammer and nails. Megan looked away from him and continued typing until she sensed him standing beside her desk, waiting without speaking. Her heart pounded although she presented a calm face as she looked up at him.

"If you'll forgive the intrusion I'll brace that screen so the unfortunate accident of this morning will not be repeated." Jacques laid his nails on the corner of her desk.

Megan jumped up so quickly that she almost overturned her chair. She felt tongue-tied as she remembered the scene that had taken place earlier, as she recalled her angry words. She had promised Yolanda to apologize, and although Yolanda had insisted an apology would be unnecessary, Megan knew her conscience would rest easier once the words had been said. She wanted no rift between them due to her bad manners.

"Mr. Ducruet?"

If Jacques heard, he did not let on.

Megan tried again. "Mr. Ducruet, I want to apologize for my behavior this morning. I was unduly upset over the small accident that took place and I hope you'll forgive me for my angry outburst. I realize that the incident was in no way your fault."

"I assure you that no apology is necessary." Jacques's words clinked like ice in a glass. He delivered them with his back to her as he stooped to examine painstakingly the legs of the teakwood screen.

"What are you doing?" Megan blurted, uneasy in the strained, velvet-padded silence that engulfed them.

"My actions should be obvious. My home has been damaged. My fault, of course. But I intend to brace this screen so this morning's accident won't be repeated while you are in residence."

Megan felt a glow begin to warm her from the inside out. So the suave, uncaring Jacques Ducruet had a compassionate side to his nature after all. And he was attached to his home. That was a surprise. Feeling ashamed of herself for having misjudged him entirely, Megan smiled and spoke again.

"I appreciate your concern for my safety, Mr. Ducruet. It is more than I deserve after the way I talked to you this morning."

Jacques hammered the brace in place with three savage blows, pounding the nail right through the carpeting. His knuckles grew white with the effort and tendons stood out in the sides of his neck. He set a second brace at a ninety degree angle to the screen before replying.

"You have completely misinterpreted my actions, Miss Taylor. Thoughts for your safety had not entered my head. My concern is for my home and my possessions, for this handsome teakwood screen." He ran a slim finger over a fresh scratch on the wood. "The screen is a family heirloom that originally came from India. You can see that this morning's episode damaged it. I'm just trying to make sure that no more harm comes to the fine wood."

"I see."

"The braces can be removed and the nailholes filled after Yolanda vacates the suite." Jacques hammered the second brace into place.

With face flaming in anger and humiliation Megan watched, speechless, as Jacques rose from his squatting position, crossed the plush carpeting, and disappeared into his private chamber, closing the door firmly behind him. For a moment she slumped in her chair, then she straightened her spine.

"You cad!" She spat the words at the closed door then continued typing. What did she care if Jacques Ducruet refused to accept her apology? After this two-week stint of working for Yolanda she would never see him again. His cavalier attitude toward her did not matter in the least.

Megan continued writing copy, but whenever she paused to think even for a moment, Jacques Ducruet's image dominated her mind. She saw the way his hands gripped the hammer, the way his fingers held the nails. His dark eyes seemed to bore into her soul, but for some reason, it was his hands that she remembered most—capable hands, strong hands, hands that she wanted to reach out and touch, and that she wanted to feel caressing her face, her arms, her body. She tried to keep her mind on cutting her copy to 200 words for each charity event, but it was hard to concentrate when a small inner voice kept reminding her that she was in Jacques Ducruet's private sitting room. How many women had he entertained here? Who were they?

When at last she finished her rough draft and typed up a final copy of the flyer, Megan paused long enough to sip a cup of coffee. Now for the easy part of the task, she thought. Assembling the names of last year's patrons and the amounts of their donations should be simple.

Megan rolled a fresh sheet of paper into the typewriter and began copying names and numbers. She had just completed the listing when she gasped, glad that she had caught her oversight before Yolanda discovered it. Jacques Ducruet's name was missing from the register of patrons. How terrible if she had let such an oversight slip by her! Surely Jacques was one of the important contributors to the Yolanda Drive. And in his present mood he surely would have thought her error intentional. Such a slight might even have cost her this job. Megan shuddered, hating to think that her future could hang on the slim thread of Jacques Ducruet's approval or disapproval.

Hurrying, Megan re-read the file Yolanda had given her, searching for Jacques's name. She studied all the material twice. Jacques's name was not among those patrons listed. Perhaps the oversight was Yolanda's error. Megan eyed the door to Jacques's private chamber. No. She could never bring herself to intrude, to ask him for the information she needed. After all, she had promised Yolanda that Jacques would not be disturbed from this quarter. After their recent exchange of words she had no desire to talk with Jacques ever again no matter what the subject.

Surely this was an emergency. Picking up the telephone Megan dialed Henri's Salon. "May I speak to Miss Delgado please?" she asked the voice on the other end of the line. "Megan Taylor calling."

"I'm sorry, Señorita Taylor," the voice replied. "Miss Delgado left here some time ago."

"Where can I reach her, please?"

"Miss Delgado did not say where she was going."

Megan sighed. "Gracias, Señor."

Megan replaced the receiver and scowled at the telephone. Now what? The figure for Jacques's donation was not in the file Yolanda had given. Yolanda was unavailable. The copy had to be ready for the printer in a very short time. Again Megan eyed the door to Jacques's private chamber. As much as she hated to, she was going to have to disturb him. She would sacrifice her pride for the sake of her job. She really had no other choice.

Taking a quick sip of coffee as if it would give her the

courage she needed to face Jacques Ducruet again, Megan crossed the room and knocked on his door. The door opened almost instantly. Jacques looked her up and down, his eyes missing no detail of her appearance, then his gaze lingered on the V of her blouse.

Megan felt her face burning and the sensation of heat grew stronger as a throaty, feminine voice called out from somewhere behind Jacques.

"Who's there, darling? You promised . . ."

Jacques scowled at Megan, then called over his shoulder, "It's nothing, love. I'll be right with you." When he turned back to Megan his eyes were blazing and angry red blotches showed through the tan on his cheeks.

Chapter Six

"I left orders that I was not to be disturbed, Miss Taylor. What major crisis has caused you to violate my wishes?"

Megan tried to make her voice as frosty as Jacques's. "I am sorry, Mr. Ducruet, but in typing up a list of charity patrons and their contributions for Yolanda's flyer I find your name missing. Perhaps you can supply the figure I need to complete the flyer before Yolanda's deadline with the printer."

Megan had expected Jacques to invite her into his room while he looked up the information she needed, but now, after hearing that he had company, she was totally confused as to what she might expect from him.

"There is a good and simple reason why you cannot

find the figure you are searching for." Jacques looked down at her with mingled amusement and irritation.

"I assure you that knocking on your private door has not made my day. I looked everywhere for the information before I bothered you."

"I'm quite sure you did." Now Jacques leaned against the door jamb with one hand, splaying his fingers in a way that again called Megan's attention to their potential strength. "You see, Miss Taylor, you cannot find the proper figure because there is no such figure to find."

"What do you mean?" Megan blinked, dumbfounded.

"Just what I said. It's quite simple. If one does not donate to a charity, then there is no figure for one's contribution available to the public."

Megan tilted her head to one side as if unable to believe she was hearing correctly. "You don't donate to the Yolanda Drive?"

"That's right, little Megan. I have never contributed cash to any charity. I lend the Ducruet name." Jacques paused for a moment. "You needn't look at me as if I just sprouted two heads. My name carries a lot of weight. The Yolanda Drive headquarters occupy my suite at the Ducruet hotel. The Ducruet plane will fly patrons to San Blas. The Ducruet yacht will take patrons fishing. The Ducruet villa will be opened for the final gala."

Megan almost choked on her indignation. "What you are saying, Mr. Ducruet, is that you only give to charity in ways that cost you little and in ways that are sure to repay you and your enterprises in full. You've found a way to have your cake and eat it too, haven't you? You have the fun of playing with all your elaborate toys, yet the advertising the famous Ducruet name receives and the business that advertising draws will more than repay you for the use of your suite, your plane, your yacht, your villa."

"I sincerely hope that is the case," Jacques said. "That is my considered plan of action."

Megan backed off and stared at Jacques as if seeing the devil himself. "I've never heard of anything so mercenary in all my life. Never!"

"I fully intend to be repaid for anything I donate to the Yolanda Drive. I'm amazed that you're so surprised. Yolanda has a clear understanding of my feelings about the matter of a contribution. Had you consulted her . . ."

Megan spluttered for a moment. "How can you be so . . . callous?"

"It isn't that I'm callous, Miss Taylor. It's just that I have a firm belief that people do not benefit from nor appreciate fully those things which they get free. Appreciation under such circumstances is contrary to human nature. A person appreciates only what he works for, not what someone, some do-gooder, hands to him on a silver platter."

Megan felt herself burning with anger. "What a ridiculous assumption!" She thought of her own education which her grandmother had paid for and which she greatly appreciated. "You are wrong, Mr. Ducruet. And what is even worse, Mr. Ducruet, you are a stingy, hard-hearted miser. All your millions! Yet your only thought is to aggrandize more wealth for Jacques Ducruet. Your shallowness astounds me!"

Without another word Megan turned and flounced back to her desk. She heard Jacques's door slam, but she ignored the sound. Sitting down at the typewriter she finished the last of the flyer copy just in time to present it to Yolanda when she returned to the suite.

"Very good," Yolanda replied as she read over the material. "It's professionally done. I'll call a messenger from the desk and have him run it to the printer for me. In the right-hand drawer of the desk you will find envelopes. You may begin typing names and addresses on them, using the same list that you used for the flyers."

"Yes, Yolanda. I should have the envelopes addressed before closing time." Megan wondered what Yolanda would say when she learned that she had disturbed Jacques that afternoon, disturbed him and asked him embarrassing questions and called him unflattering names.

"I appreciate your efficiency, Megan," Yolanda said. "Now I must leave again. I am appearing for cocktails at the Mendez mansion."

"Pablo Mendez, the designer?"

Yolanda smoothed her skirt over her hips. "It has nothing to do with the drive, but it never hurts a girl to be seen in the right places and by the right people. Close the suite at six, Megan, and enjoy a good dinner. Tomorrow will be a busier day."

"Very good, Yolanda."

Megan worked on the envelopes with mixed emotions simmering inside her. At five o'clock she decided to call Gram and report as she had promised to do.

"Glad to hear from you, Megan. How is the job going?"

"I'm delighted that Yolanda's pleased with my work, Gram, but the circumstances surrounding the drive disgust me."

"It isn't your place to criticise, Megan. Just think of the end results—the scholarships."

"Clearly, Yolanda's milking the drive for all the publicity she can get, and just as clearly Jacques Ducruet is milking it for all the free advertising he can get for the Ducruet Enterprises."

"But the scholarships will make it all worthwhile."

"That's about all that's keeping me on the job, Gram. Jacques and Yolanda are two of a kind. They deserve each other."

"Hang in there, Megan . . . I don't want to cut you short, but I have a dinner date. Call me again soon, won't you?"

"Of course, Gram." Feeling slightly deflated, Megan ended the conversation. But at least it helped to be able to tell someone exactly how she felt.

At six o'clock Megan locked the outer door to the suite and strolled to her quarters. She had heard nothing more from Jacques's private chamber and she tried to put him and his companion from her mind. She started to dial room service to have her dinner sent up, then she paused. She couldn't bear the thought of eating another meal alone on the tiny balcony no matter how grand the view of the city. She would eat downstairs in the dining room where she could at least see other people.

Peeling off her tailored working outfit, she showered and slipped into the one long gown she had brought with her, then she combed her thick hair into a French roll, securing it in place with rhinestone-studded combs. The understated elegance of the jade-green gown she had made herself set off her figure to good advantage, and she left the suite confident that she looked her best.

Megan smiled as she remembered the great satisfaction she had found in sewing some of her own clothes. She knew her body better than any dress designer, and her garments clung where they were supposed to cling and they flowed where they were supposed to flow. She walked to the elevator with assurance and she was conscious of many eyes following her as she left the lift and headed toward the open-air dining room.

"Are you dining alone, Señorita?" the hostess asked, ushering her onto a patio that overlooked the sea.

"Yes. Por favor, a secluded seat."

The hostess led the way to a table for two near a low coral-rock wall that ringed the dining area. Outside the wall palms and lime trees were silhouetted against the blaze red of the western sky as the sun dropped behind the distant hills.

"Do you care for a drink before dinner, Señorita?"

Megan started to say no, then she reconsidered. "A glass of white wine, please."

Now the tide had gone out and the harbor was quiet as a millpond. Gulls wheeled and dived for small fish while other shore birds poked along the rocky beach searching for crabs or clams. The air carried the scent of the sea along with the fragrance of plumeria and jasmine.

The hostess soon returned with both the wine and the dinner menu. Megan ordered the filet of snapper supreme in lemon butter sauce, then sipped her wine while she waited to be served. A native boy dressed in white appeared carrying a lighted taper with which he lighted the black torches that ringed the dining area and provided a flickering light for the diners. Megan watched the yellow-orange flames rise and lick toward the sky as the torches gave off curls of pewter-colored smoke.

Jacques joined Megan so swiftly and silently that she had no time to protest or to register surprise. The lime scent of his after shave awakened her senses and made her acutely aware that she enjoyed his presence more than she must ever let him realize.

"May I?" he asked after he was already seated. "I hate to see a beautiful lady dining alone."

For a split second Megan was tempted to get up and

walk out, or to ask Jacques to leave, then she reconsidered. She had made enough scenes for one day. A third one might surely cost her her job. These things were on the top of her mind, but underneath she felt flattered that Jacques Ducruet had sought her out. His mood seemed to have changed completely. They had nothing at all in common, but she could not deny that he attracted her physically, if not mentally. Why not enjoy her meal with a handsome man! Soft Panamanian evenings were not created for solitary dining.

"You will let me join you, won't you?" Jacques asked again when Megan still hadn't replied.

"If you care to," she said at last. "I would have supposed the gallant Jacques Ducruet would have many ladies waiting to dine with him. Are you sure you can spare the time for a mere secretary?"

"Still the spitfire, aren't you?" Jacques smiled across the table at her condescendingly. "I assure you that many Panamanian ladies would gladly exchange places with you right now."

"Your modesty is underwhelming," Megan replied. A breeze had come up and the torch flames leaned and danced, casting long shadows on Jacques's face that masked the expression in his eyes. Megan looked away from him, listening to the waves lapping against the shore. How handsome he looked in his dark suit! It was true, though she would never have admitted it to him, that she had noticed the eyes of other women lingering on him as he had purposefully sat down at her table. A sudden desire to reach up and touch his hand prompted her to fold her hands on her lap.

Jacques caught the waitress's attention, ordered a steak and a bottle of wine, then gave his full attention to Megan once more.

"Tell me about your young man." Jacques glanced at

her solitaire. "He surely must resent this job you have taken that keeps you from seeing him for two whole weeks."

"He will manage to survive," Megan said. "And his name is my secret. At any rate he is nobody you would know. The two of you travel in different circles."

"I see." Jacques sipped his wine, looking into Megan's eyes over the edge of his goblet. "Then tell me about yourself, Megan Taylor. Where have you been all my life and where are you going?"

"I'm sure my private life would hold little interest for you."

"You are wrong, of course. Tell me about yourself. I insist."

Megan inhaled the lime scent that wafted from Jacques's person and she softened a bit. "Really, there is little to tell. Long ago my father's people came to Panama to work on the canal. My father branched out on his own to start a much-needed tin can factory. You know the end of that story. My mother died when I was very young, and Daddy and I lived together until he . . . died. Then Gram took me in, supplemented my high school education with a year of business school, and here I am working for Yolanda Delgado."

Jacques smiled at her. "I fear you have glossed over some of the most important details of your life."

The waitress served their meal and they ate in silence for many moments. Megan hoped Jacques didn't notice the way her fingers trembled to lift her wine glass. She did not want him to think that his presence was the reason for her unsteadiness. A boy dressed in tight black pants and a ruffled white shirt strolled onto the patio playing a mandolin and singing "Spanish Eyes." Jacques slipped him a bill and he stood beside their table and sang "Celito Lindo."

"Very beautiful," Megan said when the boy wandered off. "But now perhaps it is your turn to tell me about yourself."

"Oh, I've led the usual life of a stingy miser." Jacques grinned at her. "You know how it goes."

"No, I don't know how it goes at all. Do tell me. You're the first stingy miser I've had the opportunity to meet."

"Promise to observe a temporary truce?" Jacques winked at her. "I was beginning to think you had declared open warfare on me."

"Not so. A cold war perhaps, but never a hot war. Yolanda will keep me far too busy for that."

"You have some long-time resentment against wealthy men?"

"Only stingy wealthy men."

"I cannot be bothered with wasting money on charity." Jacques sighed. "If I give to one, they'll all hound me. I pour all my profits back into the Ducruet Enterprises."

Now the wandering minstrel was singing "La Paloma." He paused at their table, looking directly at Megan as he sang. Jacques did not tip him again and when he strolled on Jacques laughed.

"The Dove!" He certainly chose the wrong lady to sing that melody to." Again they ate in silence.

After they finished their meal, Jacques pulled a small package from his jacket pocket and laid it on the table in front of Megan. Megan was more attracted by the look of his strong tan hands against the white tablecloth than by the box.

"For me?"

Jacques nodded, not taking his eyes from her. "Please do me the favor of opening it now."

Trying to steady her hands that again had started

trembling uncontrollably, Megan slipped the wrapping from the box, opened it, and gazed down at her bracelet which had been damaged that morning and which now was repaired. Before she could say anything Jacques picked the gold band from the box, slipped it around her wrist and secured it in place. Megan felt a chill feather up the whole length of her arm at his touch.

"Mr. Ducruet! How can I ever thank you?"

"Perhaps by calling me Jacques. We are going to be working together on Yolanda's charity drive for many days. We may as well try to be friends. And you could thank me by letting me show you my hotel."

"I appreciate your mending my bracelet almost more than I can say," Megan replied truthfully. "But I have seen your hotel. A tour won't be necessary." Megan avoided Jacques's gaze, knowing she might weaken in her decision if she looked into his eyes. He owed her the repair of the bracelet. She owed him nothing and she refused to let him make her feel indebted.

"You owe me nothing, Megan," Jacques said as if reading her mind. "But do let me show you the roof terrace. I had it designed especially so the music from the dance groups would drift into my suite—the Yolanda suite. Surely you noticed it last night. Come, let me take you to the terrace. Even a wealthy miser likes to show off his toys, you know."

Something warm in Jacques's manner broke through the icy barrier Megan had erected between them. What would it hurt to view the roof terrace? It was a place she could not go unescorted, and a long night lay ahead of her. She could keep her cool, keep Jacques Ducruet in his place.

"All right," she said. "You may show me the roof terrace, then I must return to my room." She almost stumbled over the last two words as she realized all too well that "her room" was really Jacques Ducruet's room, his bedroom.

They strolled from the dining area to the elevator and Jacques pushed the button that whisked the cage to the roof of the hotel. He linked his arm through Megan's as they stepped into the tropic evening. She felt the warmth of his flesh through the thin silk of his jacket. A chill feathered across the back of her neck and her arm burned under his touch.

A string group was playing latin rhythms, the breeze was wafting a jasmine scent over the dance floor, and moonlight was flooding the whole scene. Before Megan could protest Jacques eased her onto the dance floor, holding her tightly to him as their bodies flowed in rhythm with the music. Megan followed his lead faultlessly, all the time wondering if he could feel her heart pounding through the thin fabric of her gown and the equally thin fabric of his shirt.

As he pulled her more closely to him she was conscious of his hand against her back, the splayed fingers, the strength of his arm against her. Megan floated in his embrace as she had never before floated in any man's arms. The wine filled her with a heady inner warmth that was not cooled by the sea breeze. When the music ended they were standing on a palm-fringed balcony in a secluded area of the terrace.

Jacques still held her close and gradually he tilted her head back so the moonlight shone full on her face. *He's going to kiss me*, Megan thought, and although her mind shouted no, her body failed to respond to the mental command, its only response being to the warm nearness of Jacques Ducruet. As his mouth moved slowly and purposefully toward hers Megan closed her eyes and parted her lips slightly in anticipation. She waited for the warm sweetness of his mouth against hers, her body trembling in his arms.

To her surprise the expected kiss didn't materialize. Megan opened her eyes to find Jacques smiling down at her and moving his body between her and a couple on the dance floor.

"I always shy away from women who kiss on the first date," he said lightly.

Furious, Megan stepped from the circle of his arms. "I was unaware that we had a date," she said frostily.

"Then that's even worse, isn't it?" Jacques asked. "Or do you make it your habit to kiss pick-up acquaintances?"

"I hate you!" Megan spat the words at him.

Jacques grinned. "I like your spirit. Red-headed spitfires rather attract me." He grabbed her wrist and pulled her toward him again. This time Megan broke free of his grasp, ran into an open elevator, and pushed the down button before Jacques could overtake her.

Chapter Seven

Megan half expected Jacques to follow her into the elevator, but he had turned and was talking to some people. And what would she have done if he had followed her? What a fool she had been to allow him to escort her to the roof terrace! Her face still burned with anger and her hands trembled as she fumbled with her key at the door of the Yolanda suite.

Surely Jacques had a key to the suite too. The

thought made her shiver. What if he let himself into the suite, deliberately tried to humiliate her further? But no. He wouldn't dare. Yolanda also had keys to the suite. She could appear at any moment. Jacques wouldn't risk offending Yolanda. Then Megan remembered the female voice she had heard in Jacques's private chamber. Playboy. Socialite. She was glad she wore an engagement ring for protection.

Inside the suite Megan snapped on a lamp that cast only a dim glow on the velvet of the furniture and the plushness of the carpet. She hurried to her room, pulled the draperies across the sliding doors that opened onto the balcony, then turned on the light. She turned on every light in the room. Jacques Ducruet's bedroom lost all its romantic and suggestive qualities when bathed in bright lights.

Megan hung her gown on a hanger, undressed, and prepared to step into the shower. Then pausing, she removed the chain and its medallion from her wrist. Jacques had been thoughtful to have the band repaired for her. He could have laid it aside as a trinket and forgotten about it. Or he could have ordered the repairman to return it to her by messenger.

As she stood there, naked in Jacques Ducruet's dressing room, she thought for a moment that he might have some redeeming qualities. Thoughtfulness. Caring. It had been good of him to have the bracelet repaired and to bring it to her personally.

Stepping into the cold shower Megan felt the needle sharp shafts of frigid water bring her back to her senses. Jacques Ducruet had done what any normal person would do. He had damaged a piece of property and he had seen to its repair. No more. No less.

Megan finished her shower and adjusted the water to a warm flow that soothed her nerves and made her drowsy. Then stepping from the stall onto the deep fluff of the bath mat she toweled herself dry with a king-sized bath sheet, snapped off the lights, and slipped into bed. Jacques Ducruet's bed. She seldom wore a nightgown, but tonight she rose and fumbled in her suitcase until she found the gown she had felt obliged to pack because Gram had given it to her.

The silkiness of the material clung to her breasts, her hips, somehow making her feel chaste and proper. Why couldn't she forget that this bed belonged to Jacques? It was hers for two weeks and during that time he had no claim on the bed nor on her.

Megan lay awake a long time after the lights were out. Why was Jacques Ducruet trying to provoke her? For surely that was what he was doing. Perhaps he liked girls who were hard to get. Maybe her off-limits attitude was turning him on instead of off. But that was silly. Jacques was Yolanda's man. Yolanda made that clear enough. He was merely being civil to her as he would be civil to anyone Yolanda had hired to work the charity drive for her.

When Megan closed her eyes and stretched out on the cool sheets she could still see Jacques bending toward her. She could imagine the kiss he had withheld, the feel of his lips against hers. She turned over and touched the ring on her left hand. No more men in her life—that was her vow. Especially no Jacques Ducruet.

The next morning Megan awakened to the sound of clattering Panamanian buses and she was up and dressed and had eaten melon and toast on her balcony before Yolanda stirred. She had not heard Yolanda come in the night before and it surprised her to think she had slept so soundly.

"Good morning, Megan." Yolanda smiled when

Megan reported for duty. "We have a busy day ahead of us and I am pleased that you are ready for the work."

"You want the flyers to go out today, right?" Megan asked, admiring Yolanda's gray satin slacks and see-through blouse.

"Perhaps you can work on them later this afternoon," Yolanda replied. "Our plans for the morning and the early afternoon have changed. We will be flying over San Blas, then over Jacques's yacht, then we'll touch down on Contadora for lunch at the Ducruet villa. I think we need to refresh our memories by seeing these spots personally so that we may be accurate and elaborate when we describe them to the Yolanda Drive patrons."

"Shall I call the local airport and make arrangements to charter a small plane?" Megan tried to give the impression that chartering planes and flying was nothing new to her, although actually she was terrified of flying—especially in small planes.

Yolanda shook her head and lowered her eyelids. "I've made the arrangements. Jacques will be flying us in his private plane. He called his mechanic late last night and received word that the plane will be serviced and waiting for us by nine o'clock. If you are ready we will go. Bring notepad and pen, of course."

"Of course." Megan kept calm only with great effort. And the fact that her calmness required effort infuriated her. Was she upset about flying, or was she upset because Yolanda had a late date? So Yolanda had enjoyed a late date. What concern was it of hers? None. None whatsoever. She gathered her notepad and several ballpoints, tucked them into her briefcase and faced Yolanda.

"I'm ready whenever you are."

Yolanda looked Megan over. "Those are your flying clothes? Pants would be much more appropriate."

Megan felt herself flushing. "This is the best I can do unless I have time to go shopping. I thought skirts and blouses would be most appropriate for the work I would be doing. I couldn't guess that flying was in the picture for me."

"It's hard always to know what is appropriate where Jacques is concerned," Yolanda said coolly. Her gaze went to Megan's wrist. "I see that Jacques has repaired your medallion for you."

"Yes."

"And delivered it personally, I presume?"

Megan hated herself for feeling that she had to explain personal matters to Yolanda, yet she tried to explain. "Jacques and I met by accident and he just happened to have the medallion with him, so . . ."

"Many girls have accidents when dealing with Jacques." Yolanda grinned. "Let's go."

They took a taxi for the five-minute ride to the local airport. Inside the crowded terminal building a mob of people waited. Ladies with babies. Men in business suits. Teens with tennis racquets in canvas cases.

The room was hot and stuffy and reeked of stale cigarette smoke and sweat. Heads turned when Yolanda entered, and Megan's spirits drooped when she saw that all the chairs were taken. They would have to stand.

But she was wrong. She had underestimated Jacques. A handsome man dressed in white shirt and dark pants approached Yolanda.

"Miss Delgado?"

"Yes?"

"This way, please. Mr. Ducruet is waiting for take-off."

Megan followed Yolanda and the uniformed man to the runway where Jacques Ducruet sat at the controls of a twin-engine Cessna. When he saw them approaching he climbed from the cockpit, dropped to the runway, and held out his hand to Yolanda in greeting. Ignoring the hand, Yolanda grabbed his arm possessively.

Megan's face froze but she felt her pulse pounding at her temples. Jacques was dressed in white; shirt, slacks, shoes. Surely, he was aware of the perfect foil the costume made for his golden tan. His dark eyes surveyed Megan mockingly and she thought for a moment that he was going to wink at her, but he didn't.

"Shall we go?" Jacques asked. "Other planes are waiting for us to take off." -

"Of course." Yolanda stepped forward, the sun shimmering on her satin slacks where they encased the rounded contours of her hips. Then she stood aside. "Megan, you go first. You will be sitting behind us."

Jacques took Megan's hand and helped her up the portable steps and into the plane. She felt the strength in his hand, but when she looked at him she found that his gaze was on her legs. Self-consciously she tried to gather her skirt around her knees, but it was impossible to board the plane without using both hands for pulling herself up from the ground.

Still clinging to Jacques's hand she entered the plane, seated herself behind the cockpit, and tucked her skirt around her knees. Jacques was watching and enjoying her every move, and this time when she looked at him he did wink. Before she could give him a disapproving frown he had turned to help Yolanda into the plane, then he climbed aboard himself.

"It's good of you to fly us around today, Jacques." Yolanda laid a hand on his arm and he did nothing to discourage her touch. Megan tried not to imagine her own hand on Jacques's arm, but her fingers tingled at the thought. She remembered all too vividly the warm flesh that she had felt through his silk jacket when they had danced beneath the moonlight to the scent of jasmine. She turned her gaze resolutely to the window to watch the last passengers straggle off one of the commercial planes.

"This trip's to my advantage, Yolanda," Jacques was saying. "I want to be sure that you and Megan are able to describe San Blas, the yacht, my villa to the best of your ability. It will be good advertising for Ducruet Enterprises as well as for the Yolanda Drive."

In spite of her fear of flying, Megan continued to peer through the window, watching Panama City grow smaller and smaller as they gained altitude. She saw the Old City, the race track, then soon they were flying over jungle where the tangled vegetation was so dense she could not glimpse the ground. She looked away from the dizzying vastness below feeling lightheaded and faint.

"How shall we describe this scenic flight, Megan?" Yolanda raised her voice above the roar of the plane engines.

"A dense growth of tropical trees?" Megan suggested, trying to hide her uneasiness.

"How about the mysterious emerald green of the tropical rain forest?" Jacques asked.

Yolanda smiled up at Jacques and patted his thigh. "That's a much better description." Then turning to Megan, "Did you get that down, Megan? The Yolanda plane . . . I think that's what we will call the Cessna . . . the Yolanda plane will fly patrons over the mysterious emerald green of the tropical . . ."

"Make that the Ducruet plane, Megan," Jacques said.

"I have it down," Megan replied.

"Fine," Yolanda said. "Now jot down any other impressions you get."

Jacques flew at a lower altitude, and at times Megan felt as if she could count the fronds on the palm trees below. They flew over a brown river which snaked through the jungle, and she tried not to look down. She fought the dizziness that threatened to make her ill. After about a half hour they reached the sea.

"Ah!" Yolanda breathed the word and again she laid her hand on Jacques's thigh. "The Caribbean. I think the Caribbean Sea is the most romantic of all the waters in the world. Don't you agree?"

Jacques smiled down at her. "If you say so, Yolanda."

"I say so." Yolanda patted Jacques's thigh once more, then turned to Megan. "Let us hear your description of the sea, Megan."

"The azure waters of the Caribbean rise and froth around palm-studded islands . . ."

Jacques interrupted. "How about this . . . the blue-green swells of a sea, once the stronghold of pirates and freebooters, now welcomes visitors to the peaceful San Blas islands where the Cuna Indians live much as they have lived for centuries."

"Wonderful, Jacques," Yolanda said. "Did you get it all down, Megan? It's good to have the masculine viewpoint, isn't it?" She smiled appreciatively at Jacques.

"Of course, Yolanda." While anger churned inside her Megan vowed not to offer any more descriptions for Yolanda's criticism. She would merely take dictation from Jacques. She was not a creative writer, and clearly, Jacques would be dictating what they would say to the charity patrons.

Now they were flying over small islands that looked like green jewels set in the sea. Jacques dropped altitude again, buzzing so close to the island that the natives spilled from their thatched huts to gather on the shoreline, staring up at the plane and shielding their eyes from the sun. Megan's knuckles turned white as she gripped the armrest on her seat.

"Are we going to land?" Yolanda asked Jacques.

"Not today. I have no landing permission from the natives. But there are binoculars in the seat pockets. Use them. You can get a good general description of the island from this altitude. Today must be laundry day. See the pants and shirts flapping on that line high above the huts. The women pull the clothes up there to catch the breeze, but they lower them when tourists approach."

"How picturesque." Yolanda grinned. "I wish we could take our patrons to some of the islands that white man has never visited. That would be a real first for the Yolanda Drive. We could raise our price expectation on such an outing."

"If you had a star you'd want the moon, wouldn't you?" Jacques smiled down at Yolanda. "We're quite lucky that the Cunas have decided to open any of their islands to visitors. How would you like strangers peering into your private home?"

"They'll do anything for the money," Yolanda said scornfully.

"Can't think of a better reason," Jacques said. "Money makes the world go around."

"Love, Jacques," Yolanda corrected. "It's love that makes the world go around," she cooed.

Megan scowled. Love? Money? What did make the world go around? She could remember when she thought it was love. But after her treatment from Vance she was no longer so innocent, and surely Yolanda wasn't either. Maybe Jacques was right. Perhaps money was what made the world go around. At least it was probably what made his world go around. For a moment Megan felt sorry for the Cunas. For centuries they had lived a private existence and now, for money, they had opened their islands to the scrutiny of tourists.

They had given up their privacy and what had they gained? What did their new-found money buy them?

"Money can buy good things," Jacques said.

Could this man read her mind, Megan wondered. But she said nothing.

"With money the Cunas can get better health care, better education for their children, labor-saving devices for their people." Jacques peered at the island below them. "I like to think that by opening their islands to outsiders they are taking a giant step forward."

Megan didn't even try to decide whether or not Jacques was right. Through the binoculars she just looked down on the island they were flying above and forgot her fear of flying for the moment as she drank in its beauty. Laundry flapped in the breeze, blue jeans, bright shirts, pastel blouses. Bare-bodied boys splashed in the surf while green parrots preened on the branches of a banana tree. On the other side of the island she saw a ramp leading to a biffy built out over the water, and a little farther on she spied a thatch-roofed pig pen also built over the water. Picturesque to say the least. She grinned. The Cunas had their own system of labor-saving devices.

The plane rose, responding like a woman to Jacques's touch, and soon the islands were far distant. Once more they looked like green spangles on a vast blue setting.

"You will fly us over your yacht, won't you?" Yolanda asked as they headed back toward Panama. "I have never seen it from the air . . ."

Megan bristled then relaxed. So Yolanda had seen the yacht from a closer vantage point. So what? Why did she care? She didn't care. She *wouldn't* care.

Chapter Eight

The flight to the Pacific side of Panama was uneventful. Megan refrained from peering from the window. Instead she busied herself by transcribing some of her shorthand notes into longhand to save time later. She tried to blot out the conversation between Yolanda and Jacques, but she kept hearing Yolanda talking about Yolanda. How she loves the sound of her name, Megan thought.

Megan didn't look up from her work until she felt the plane banking and circling. She forced herself to look down as Jacques spoke.

"There she is—*The Golden Dolphin.*"

Megan heard the pride in Jacques's voice as they circled lower and lower. Men aboard the yacht waved their gold-colored caps at the plane and Jacques dipped a wing in response. Megan clung to the plane seat, her knuckles growing white from strain.

"She's a beaut, isn't she?" Jacques asked, looking at Yolanda. "Sixty feet of sleekness. Complete kitchen. Complete bar. And she'll sleep twelve easily. But, of course you know all that already don't you, Yolanda."

"I prefer your secluded house in Colón, Jacques." Yolanda lowered her lashes then peered up at Jacques with a sidelong glance. "Places that sleep only two are more to my liking."

"Perhaps there is safety in numbers, my dear."

Megan ignored the banter, staring at the gleaming white yacht with its gold-colored sails. The color of money, she thought. Even the sailors manning the craft wore gold-colored pants and shirts. But she had to admit that the craft was beautiful and impressive and she did her best to put a vivid description on paper.

"I love to see the whitecaps frothing against the sides of the yacht," Jacques said. "They have a hypnotic effect on me. It's like time itself is stored in deep layers in the sea."

Yolanda leaned toward Jacques until their shoulders touched. "You are very poetic. When I look long enough I can hypnotize myself into thinking I am lying on a water bed. The gentle motion. Rocking. Rocking."

"I had forgotten you were so fond of water beds," Jacques said dryly. Then he straightened the plane and in moments they circled the island of Contadora and landed on the small palm-bordered airstrip.

"Jacques, you should have circled more of the Pearl Islands," Yolanda said. "Megan's probably never seen them before, have you, Megan?"

Megan bristled. Why did Yolanda assume that she had never been anywhere, never seen anything? "Oh, I've visited Contadora now and then when my father was alive, Yolanda. It's a lovely place."

Jacques eased past Yolanda, bracing his hand for an instant on her knee, then he opened the door of the plane and lowered himself to the ground. Megan inhaled the scent of plumeria and felt the warm moist air against her face. She hadn't been aware of how much Jacques's plane reeked of Yolanda's gardenia scent.

An attendant rolled portable steps into place then Jacques helped Yolanda alight. Megan stalled, closing her notebook, placing her pens carefully in her brief-case. She felt sweat beading on her upper lip. Perhaps

Jacques would go on with Yolanda and let her get out of the plane under her own power. But that was not to be.

"Do hurry, Megan," Yolanda called. "This sun is broiling hot and Jacque's man is waiting for us with the car."

Stooping slightly, Megan stepped to the doorway and gazed down into Jacques's eyes. The ground seemed to swim up to meet her.

"Take my hand, Megan. Let me help you down."

Megan wanted to look away, but Jacques's eyes held her captive. She could sense that Yolanda was pacing in the background and her brain told her to move quickly, to alight, to get on with the business of the day. But when Jacques took her hand her body refused to hurry. She allowed him to help her from the plane although she said nothing but a murmured thank you. She felt as if she were being pulled in two different directions at the same time. Her mind was telling her to ignore Jacques while her body seemed bent on keeping the two of them together.

Now Jacques linked one arm through Yolanda's and the other through Megan's and steered them toward the waiting Mercedes that matched the car Jacques used in Panama. Megan felt as though her arm had developed a giant pulse where it touched Jacques's, and the pounding unnerved her. She was sure she could hear it, and was afraid that Jacques could too. Suddenly she wished that she could throw both arms around his neck in a passionate embrace that would shut Yolanda away from them completely. . . . Jacques's casual greeting to his driver interrupted Megan's daydream.

"*Buenos días,* José," Jacques called to the driver.

"*Buenos días,* Señor." José's voice flowed like wine, full-bodied and smooth.

"You ride in front with José," Jacques said to

Yolanda when they reached the car. "I want to be able to point out special scenic spots to Megan so she can capture them on paper. She may have seen Contadora before, but she certainly hasn't seen my private estate and that's what the patrons will want to know all about."

Yolanda scowled, but she slid onto the front seat with the driver. A whale of a man, José gave Megan the impression of great strength. His barrel chest and his muscled shoulders strained at the seams of his white on white embroidered sport shirt. The strong stench of his black cigar hung in the Mercedes. He ground the cigar out in the ash tray as he flashed Jacques a knowing smile. Then he stared straight ahead after the introductions were completed.

Jacques helped Megan into the back seat then slid in beside her. Now his sardonic grin was absent and he was straight-faced and businesslike.

"Drive us directly to the villa, José," Jacques said. "I hope lunch has been prepared for us. I'm sure both these ladies are starving."

"*Sí*, Señor. My Juanita take special pains with the lunch for Miss Yolanda. Miss Yolanda one of her favorite people."

"And Juanita is the best cook I know," Yolanda said. "Excluding Jacques, of course."

Megan looked out the window. Palms and seagrape grew to the edge of the airstrip and there was not enough breeze to stir a hair until José drove up onto the winding road that rose and curved until they overlooked the sea splashing over dark boulders then rolling onto the pebbled beach. As the car rounded the bends in the road, Megan was thrown against Jacques. Although she had tucked her skirt carefully around her legs, she felt the warmth of Jacques's thigh against her own. She pretended not to notice their bodies touching, but her cheeks flamed and her skin tingled. She did not know how to pull away without calling attention to herself, so she sat as bolt upright as she could, inhaling the clean, heady scent of Jacques's cologne, dizzy with the touch of the dark jaw that had just grazed her hair. If Jacques was conscious of their proximity or her response to it, he gave no sign. Yolanda's reaction, however, was obvious.

"Slow down," she said sharply to José. "My secretary is trying to take notes on the terrain as we drive along. Surely there is no big hurry to reach the villa."

"I thought the señor was in a hurry." José slowed the car a bit, and Megan eased away from Jacques as she pulled her notepad and pen from her briefcase and tried to make some legible comments on what she was seeing.

"Be sure to mention the white sand beach," Jacques said.

Megan looked up at him in amazement. "I see no such beach. All I see is that rocky shoreline and the caramel-colored sand where the gulls are feeding. I won't lie to the patrons."

"Nobody is asking you to lie, Miss Taylor." The twinkle in Jacques's eyes belied the frost in his voice, and the next time Megan glanced from the window she saw a secluded cove, a white sand beach, and water so clear she thought it might be a hallucination.

"Oh! How lovely!" Megan leaned forward for a better look and her thigh touched Jacques's. She moved away quickly, sensing his silent laughter.

"My bedroom window overlooks that cove," Jacques said. "You should see it in the moonlight."

"But our guests will have no access to your bedroom," Yolanda said icily. "Let us keep to the business of the day, please. We have but little time here and I want Megan to capture the elusive spirit of the villa estate."

"Of course, Yolanda." Jacques leaned forward, tapping José on the shoulder. "A little faster, José. The lady is in a hurry to reach our destination."

José stepped on the gas and again Megan felt her body sway toward Jacques. She felt his arm go around her shoulders in a steadying, protective gesture. Again, she felt anger burning inside her. Or was it desire? Jacques was teasing both her and Yolanda. Teasing in an infuriating way. He was using her to make Yolanda jealous and in turn he was using Yolanda to try to make her jealous. Cad. She touched the ring on her engagement finger as a silent reminder to Jacques that she was spoken for. But her gesture didn't quite come off as she wished. She suspected that he had guessed that the ring was a false symbol.

They passed the Contadora Hotel which displayed bright bunting over its gateway welcoming Sun Tours of Canada. Yellow buses and a few private cars dotted the hotel parking lot. People were lunching at an open-air bar near the pool while a guitarist serenaded them with latin melodies.

"There's an excellent casino at the hotel," Jacques said. "Perhaps you ladies would like to visit it before we leave the island."

"Of course not," Yolanda snapped. "Really, Jacques, this is a business trip. If I feel an urge to gamble I will do it at Hotel Ducruet where I am known and respected."

They passed many island hideaways including the house in which Jacques said the canal treaties had been signed. Then they rounded another curve in the road and there Jacques's villa stood dominating a headland that overlooked the sea. It was a huge, rambling structure, and the siding was weathered to a warm brown that bespoke of salt air and sunshine. The roof appeared to be thatched, but on closer examination Megan could see that the thatch was merely a picturesque cover for a more conventional roof underneath.

José stopped in front of the entryway where a brown lattice framing formed a philodendron and ivy shrouded tunnel that led into the shaded recesses of the villa. Now Yolanda took Jacques's arm while Megan followed them, feeling like their pet spaniel at heel.

As Megan's heels clattered against the bare teakwood floors, she admired the pots of exotic palms and cacti that gave color to the corners of the spacious room. A faint scent of lemon oil hung in the room as if someone had recently finished polishing the furniture or the floor.

Cool bamboo furniture with jewel-toned cushions had been placed artistically around the room to invite lingering, but Jacques led them on to an open-air patio. Here a bamboo table shaded by a yellow umbrella had been set for two, and Megan saw a reed-thin woman of middle years waiting in a doorway that she guessed led into the kitchen. The woman wore a scowl as black as her uniform as she hurried toward Jacques. Her dark eyes snapped, belying her honey-smooth words.

"Beg pardon, Señor." She bowed nervously, twisting the wide gold wedding band on her left hand. "We were expecting only a party of two as usual. Un momento. I will set another place."

"Fine, Juanita. This is Miss Megan Taylor, Yolanda's charity drive secretary."

Juanita bowed to Megan and then turned and almost ran to the kitchen. In moments she was back with another place setting for the table. She reminded Megan of a cricket, full of nervous energy and determined to use every bit of it.

"Please to be seated." Juanita gestured toward the table.

Jacques led the way, but Megan made certain that Yolanda sat between her and Jacques. It wasn't a difficult maneuver. Yolanda had the same idea.

Megan jotted notes concerning the living room decor and the shaded patio as they waited to be served.

"Mention the living room will serve as a ballroom for the gala," Jacques said. "And it won't hurt to stress the moon-silvered patio with its view of the beach."

Megan hadn't seen the beach yet from this patio. There had been too much confusion at first, and now that they were seated her back was to the view.

Juanita served lobster in lemon butter and thin circles of French-fried plantains. When they had enjoyed these delicacies, she appeared with a fruit cup dessert. Papaya, melon, orange slices, all drenched in a special sweet-tart syrup and laced with champagne. Megan had never tasted such a delightful meal.

After they finished eating, Yolanda excused herself. "I want to talk with Juanita about the refreshments for the gala. She'll need extra kitchen and serving help, of course."

"Of course," Jacques said. "Whatever you and she agree on will be fine with me. I know your taste in such matters is faultless."

As Yolanda left them Jacques winked at Megan who pretended not to notice. What was in a wink? They certainly were not conspirators in any sense of the word. Ignoring Jacques, Megan left the table and wandered to the low stone ledge between the patio and the sloping path down to the beach. As she stood gazing at the placid cove which ranged in color from light green at the beach to cobalt blue some distance from shore, Jacques joined her linking his arm through hers. Megan immediately eased from his touch; she did not want him to feel her all too eager response to the firm, warm flesh against her own.

"How dare you . . . after last night . . ." Words failed her and she felt foolish and exposed. Jacques knew that she had expected him to kiss her, that she had been willing. Even now she could imagine his lips against her own, giving and demanding.

"How dare I what?" Jacques asked. "I'm not trying to seduce you, little spitfire. I'm only trying to protect my property in a diplomatic manner." Jacques pointed toward the ground where Megan was accidentally stepping on the leaf of an exotic plant.

"You are about to tread on my bird-of-paradise," Jacques said. "I was merely trying in a subtle way to guide your footsteps elsewhere. I've spent a lot of time nurturing that plant and now that it is about to bloom . . ."

"Oh, Jacques! I'm sorry. I really didn't see it." Megan stooped to examine the leaf she had crushed, smelling the yeasty scent of the foliage. "I hope I haven't damaged the plant permanently. The bud is unharmed." She lifted the bud with her fingertip.

"I'm sure it will be all right if it receives no further punishment." Jacques looked down at her neither smiling nor frowning and Megan rose.

"If the plant dies I will replace it for you. It was clumsy of me to step on it. I was mesmerized by the view." Megan held her chin high, regaining her composure.

"I don't understand you, Megan. One minute you are warm and compassionate over a damaged plant and the next minute you are all frost and ice again."

Megan heard the mockery in his voice and turned to go back to the table, but Jacques slid an arm around her waist and pulled her to the low wall beside him. She slipped from his touch, but she remained standing by the wall, not trusting her legs to carry her the distance back to the table, not trusting herself to look at Jacques.

"Are you still angry about the kiss you missed out on last night, Megan?"

Seething inside Megan looked away and said nothing. Was any job worth the anger and frustration she was feeling?

"I am angry about it also," Jacques said, laughter bubbling in his voice. "And I intend to make amends at the earliest opportunity. But, you see, I truly was acting in your behalf last night. At the moment you closed your eyes for my kiss I spotted a couple on the dance floor well known to Yolanda and myself. It would have been unwise for me to let them see us in a compromising situation. Yolanda has fired secretaries out of pure jealousy before. You would not be the first."

Still Megan did not answer—could not answer. She did not trust herself to voice her feelings when her feelings were in such a turmoil. How could she hate a man and at the same time want him? Surely he was playing her against Yolanda, tantalizing her with Yolanda's near presence and Yolanda's position of authority over her.

"Your job with the Yolanda Drive is very important to you, isn't it?"

"It is everything to me, Mr. Ducruet," Megan replied, holding her voice steady. "Everything."

"I can understand that, Megan. If there is anything I admire in a girl it is a practical nature. We musn't do anything to jeopardize your position, right?"

Megan looked at Jacques to find him devouring her with his eyes as he had done the first time they met. His gaze disconcerted her and she looked away quickly, hating herself for letting Jacques intimidate her.

"Of course next to a practical nature I admire ladies with red hair, beautiful faces and figures, and enough cleavage showing to allow me to dream a little."

Megan didn't hear Yolanda return. She actually felt her presence. She guessed that Jacques felt it too because they both turned at the same time to find Yolanda standing in the cool shadows of the kitchen doorway watching them. How long had she been there? What had she overheard?

Jacques smiled and hurried to Yolanda's side, spilling out plans for the coming gala, but Megan saw Yolanda scowling at her and for the first time she really feared for her job. Her whole future could be decided by Yolanda's whim. Megan stiffened her spine and made a pretense of jotting notes in her book. She would not put herself in a position where Jacques could jeopardize her future ever again.

Chapter Nine

The flight back to Panama was uneventful. Jacques flew out of his way to pass over the Miraflores Locks and the canal, and Megan forced herself to look down at the lineup of ships waiting to pass through the waterway. But her mind was not on ships and canals. Her mind was on her job and the relationship between Jacques and Yolanda that might put her job in danger.

Jacques looked at the spectacular sight below, but Yolanda ignored the scene, chattering about plans for the gala as well as plans for the other charity events. As soon as they left the canal area Megan looked up and kept her eyes on her notebook for the rest of the trip. She was glad that Yolanda didn't read shorthand. At least she would never know exactly what notes Megan had taken or had not taken.

Jacques drove them from the airport to Hotel Ducruet and escorted them to the door of the Yolanda Suite. Although Megan mentally prepared herself for a reprimand from Yolanda concerning her behavior with Jacques at the villa, none was forthcoming. Yolanda was businesslike but friendly as she outlined the rest of the day's duties.

"I want these flyers in the mail this evening, Megan. It may rush you, but do see that it is accomplished. After you finish stuffing the envelopes, take them downstairs to the main desk. Ask for messenger service, then direct the boy to deliver the flyers to the post office personally. Do you understand? It is most important to the drive."

Megan inhaled the fresh-off-the-press smell of the flyers. "Yes, Yolanda. I'll see that this material gets in the mail today. Don't worry about it."

"Then I will depend on you." Yolanda glanced at her watch. "Now I have an appointment at Henri's Salon. In case you need to consult me about anything, I'll be there. I will not be returning to the suite until quite late this evening as I have a dinner engagement."

"Fine, Yolanda." Megan felt the slickness of the flyers as she began folding them and inserting them into the envelopes. The glue on the envelope flaps tasted like lime, not at all unpleasant. Megan wondered if Yolanda had arranged this. Could the wealthy even control the glue on envelope flaps?

"I hope you will find it convenient to take your dinner in the suite," Yolanda said. "I may need to telephone you about details."

"Of course, Yolanda. I'll be here all evening."

"You will have dinner sent up?"

"Is that an order?" Megan spoke more sharply than she had intended to. She tried to soften her words with a smile.

"It is not an order, Megan." Yolanda smiled back, knowingly. "I am just trying to be sure of your whereabouts . . . in case I need to get in touch with you for anything concerning the drive. Of course you may dine wherever you please—within the hotel. I can always have you paged if I find it necessary."

Megan continued stuffing the envelopes, but now she felt sure that Yolanda knew she had dined with Jacques the evening before. Did Yolanda have spies working for her? Then a horrible thought came to mind. Perhaps Yolanda's information came directly from Jacques.

Megan stiffened in her chair as she imagined Jacques and Yolanda discussing her, amused at the poor little secretary agog at having dinner with THE Jacques Ducruet. From now on she would avoid Jacques at all costs. He might be laughing over his acquisition of Taylor Tin. She could do nothing about that, but she would give him no more reason to laugh at Megan Taylor personally.

Yolanda soon left the suite in a flurry of swishing satin and directions tossed over her shoulder. Now Megan faced the stack of envelopes and flyers alone. But she didn't mind in the least. The busy day began to tell on her. The back of her neck ached and she longed to relax over a glass of wine and a light supper. Chilled avocado soup? Perhaps. But not yet. She had a job to do and she had a deadline. She mustn't let Yolanda down, mustn't give her any reason to fire her for lack of performance.

It was after seven o'clock when she sealed the last

envelope and stored the extra flyers in a desk drawer. She started to call the desk and have someone come up for the mailing, then she reconsidered. If she really wanted to be efficient she would take the flyers downstairs personally, contact a messenger, and make the arrangements for the flyers to be delivered to the post office within the hour.

Megan stacked the envelopes into the box the flyers had come in, left the suite, and took the elevator to the lobby. A bellboy came to her aid and she made arrangements for the mailing. When she turned to go back to the Yolanda suite she saw Jacques standing nearby. He was studying the wall hanging of Cuna molas and she would have to pass close to him in order to reach the elevator.

Megan walked purposefully toward the lift, half expecting Jacques to stop her, but when she passed him he merely looked up, nodded rather absently, and continued his scrutiny of the molas.

Megan stepped into the elevator and returned to the Yolanda suite.

"I'm glad, glad, glad that he made no attempt to join me," Megan said aloud, conscious of the velvet absorbing her words. But even as she spoke, she was conscious of a let-down feeling. Grabbing the telephone she dialed room service. "I'd like a glass of white wine, chilled soup, and a tossed salad sent up, please."

She paced until the supper arrived, then she carried it to her balcony where she could watch the city lights come on, turning the night into a jeweled fairyland.

To her left was a residential area, and as she watched the glowing lights gleaming from behind sheer draperies she tried to imagine the warm family scenes unfolding in the homes. Family. Husband. Children. Would that dream ever be hers? She wanted it for her own. Although she might pretend otherwise, she wanted it.

She pictured herself in a flowing hostess gown and Jacques in a satin smoking jacket as they sat on the patio of his home on Colón. The children were in bed. The maid was preparing dinner, and Jacques was sharing humorous incidents from his day with her. She imagined that they were dining in the moonlight, their eyes meeting over the rims of their wine goblets, their fingers touching as they passed the salt, the bread plate. . . . The zoom of an airplane disturbed her daydream.

As she sat alone Megan thought of her father, her grandmother, Vance. Maybe this was what nighttime was for, for thinking over the past and trying to make some sense of it. But when she looked above the city lights at the crescent moon and the stars she knew that nighttime was really for lovers. It was for people planning a lifetime together. It was for people who had found each other. The moon and stars held little charm for those whose only goal was success in the business world.

Megan carried her tray inside and although it was early she prepared for bed. What else was there to do? When she snapped off her light the pale moon glowed through the glass doors. Men had walked on that moon. And she was sleeping alone in Jacques Ducruet's bed. She lived in a crazy world. She could not control that world, but perhaps if she really tried she could control her reaction to it.

The next morning Yolanda was all business and she never mentioned her dinner engagement or her evening. Megan wondered. Had Yolanda been with Jacques? She tried not to wonder. Today Yolanda was wearing a dress of cinnamon-colored raw silk accented with silver and coral bracelets. A single silver comb gleamed at the base of her upswept hairdo. Megan sensed that Yolanda was very conscious of her looks. As usual, her awareness made Megan aware also.

"Today our work will be most important to the success of the Yolanda Drive," Yolanda said, gazing directly at Megan. "I do hope you are refreshed and rested. Perhaps you had the forethought to retire early."

"What will we do today?" Megan ignored Yolanda's invitation to reveal the details of her evening.

"The flyers have been mailed?"

"Of course. I sent them out last night as you ordered."

"Thank you. I'm glad I have a dependable secretary. Today you must write up a letter and another flyer that will sell our wealthy male patrons on the idea of a fishing trip aboard Jacques's yacht."

"I know very little about yachts and fishing. But I'll try to make *The Golden Dolphin* sound as attractive as it is."

"Of course the fishing trip idea has been discreetly leaked to the proper people, but now we are trying for the actual sale of the idea, the letter that will immediately bring in large contributions. I have jotted down idea suggestions which Jacques has approved." Yolanda laid a yellow sheet of notes on Megan's desk.

So she was with Jacques again last night, Megan thought. And she guessed that their whole evening together had not been spent discussing fishing trips and jotting notes on yellow tablet paper.

Megan tried to focus her attention on the suggestions Yolanda had given her, but the heady scent of gardenia perfume distracted her. Was that Jacques's favorite scent, she wondered. He had told her he loved roses.

Idly she wished she had some rose-scented perfume or cologne.

"May women go on the fishing trip too?" Megan asked, "Or is it strictly for men?"

Yolanda shrugged. "I suppose women may go if they want to. Their money is as good as any. But the trip is really more for the men. A macho thing, you know. Keep the letter brief but colorful. Also the flyer. Use words that carry some clout. Brief. Eye-catching. Enticing."

"You will be here later to check over the rough copy?" Megan asked.

Yolanda shook her head. "I have a busy day ahead of me. If I had planned to hang around the office, I would have had no need for a secretary. You will find the proper words. I have confidence in your abilities."

Was it the gardenia scent that was beginning to make her head ache? Megan re-read Yolanda's notes, trying to make out the scrawled handwriting.

"I will spend this morning at the dressmakers. She is to have my costumes finished—the ones I will wear on the TV show this night."

"Oh!" Megan was genuinely impressed. "What TV program will you be appearing on? I want to be sure to watch it."

"The late, late extravaganza." Yolanda laughed. "The polls show that it has quite a following among the wealthy. At any rate I will be in rehearsal for the show from mid-afternoon on. I just hope the dressmaker can make me presentable in time."

"I'm sure she will." Megan could not imagine Yolanda being unpresentable, nor could she imagine any dressmaker failing to meet a Yolanda deadline.

Yolanda checked her watch. "Oh, I must run, my dear. If you finish the yacht and fishing letter and the flyer, start on copy advertising the San Blas trip and the Contadora gala. Okay?"

"Fine, Yolanda. You won't be back today?"

"No. Mind the phone. Answer the door. You'll do well on your own." Yolanda smiled. "I have no time for coming back here. Tomorrow morning first thing I will check your work and we will see to the quick printing and the mailing. Do your best for me, little Megan. You will be amply rewarded."

"Of course, Yolanda. I'll start on the letters right away, working carefully from your notes."

The minute Yolanda was gone Megan hurried to the sliding doors, opened them wide, and let the fresh air blowing in from the harbor dilute the gardenia scent that still clung to the room. Then she relaxed. She should have a pleasant day of working alone with no interruptions from Yolanda.

If only she could write the correct things in the come-on letters, words that would draw an instant response from the charity patrons. Her business school had stressed shorthand and typing, the use of office machines. There had been no emphasis on creative writing and advertising. She knew that composing the letters to Yolanda's satisfaction would be a difficult task.

By ten o'clock Megan had drafted half a dozen letters, none of which suited her. She had entertained five patrons, telling them of the upcoming charity activities and she had answered numerous telephone calls. When another knock sounded on the door, she checked to see that tea and coffee were ready to serve, then she answered the summons.

"Good morning, Megan." Jacques looked down at her and smiled. "You're looking exceptionally fit today."

"Good morning." Megan refused to say his name, yet she was conscious of the way he had said hers. Megan. He made it sound like an endearment. "May I help you? I'm sorry, but Yolanda is out for the day."

"I just stopped by to pick up a portfolio from my private office."

Jacques strode across the room, and Megan watched the way his muscled shoulders strained against the mint green fabric of his shirt. Was there any color that would not accentuate his marvelous tan? Today he wore green slacks and deck shoes with an open-throated sport shirt. It was hardly a proper costume for a serious and successful businessman, Megan thought.

Megan returned to her desk and her letters, but when Jacques left his office he stopped near her chair and waited until she looked up.

"How is the Yolanda Drive progressing?"

Megan tried not to scowl. Jacques made Yolanda's name sound like a caress too. It was just his way. But he did sound genuinely interested in her work. But before she could answer him a troubling thought snapped into her mind. Why hadn't Jacques used his private entrance into his office? Why had he come through this way? Had Yolanda sent him to check on her work?

"Well, how *is* the drive coming along?" Jacques repeated his question. "You seem disturbed."

"Frankly, I'm having trouble composing a letter describing the fishing expedition." Megan pointed to the sheaf of rough-draft copies on her desk. "If you'd care to read what I've written perhaps you'd be able to make some suggestions. You seem to have a knack with words."

"Thank you, Megan."

"I need more facts." Megan continued quickly, not sure whether or not Jacques was making fun of her.

"For instance, how many men can fish at once? Will lunch be supplied? If the men catch fish will they be able to have them prepared for eating aboard the yacht? And what about having an unusual catch mounted? I don't want to promise more than we intend to deliver. But on the other hand, I don't want to promise less either."

The sardonic smile returned to Jacques's lips, and Megan looked away confused and irritated. But when she glanced at Jacques again he was intent on reading the copy she had written. When he finished reading, he laid the sheets down and shook his head.

"What you need is a personal tour of *The Golden Dolphin*, Megan. You're trying to write about something you don't know about."

"I saw the yacht from the air only yesterday. I was duly impressed."

"But you were frightened of the plane ride, weren't you? Flying scares you, right?"

Megan felt herself blushing. Could she hide nothing from this man? "I thought yesterday's outing was very informative."

"Come with me to the yacht today, Megan." Jacques glanced at his watch. "Come right now and we'll tour the craft. You can see the fishing chairs, the galley, the crew's quarters—everything."

"I promised Yolanda that I'd stay right here while she's away. I have no intention of losing this job through negligence to my duties."

"You'd rather lose it through poor work performance?"

"What do you mean by that?"

"Just what I said. I'm not inviting you for a pleasure outing, Miss Taylor. I'm asking you to tour my yacht because I expect better advertising coverage from the

Yolanda Drive than you've produced here." Jacques tapped a forefinger against the letters for emphasis. "This will be a business trip. You flatter yourself if you think of it as anything else. I will vouch for the way you've spent your work time if Yolanda questions you."

Infuriated, Megan struggled for polite words. "I can't leave the suite. If Yolanda had wanted me to visit the yacht she would have made those arrangements. If the copy does not suit her when she reads it, she may make any changes she finds necessary."

"You really believe that?"

"Yolanda plans to check over my work tomorrow morning before it goes to the printer."

To Megan's surprise Jacques laughed. "Yolanda make changes? She speaks English fairly well, but when it comes to writing it she's a lost ball in high weeds. And these letters should go out in Spanish as well as English. Yolanda just can't handle that. That's why she hired a bi-lingual secretary."

Megan was about to protest again, but Jacques silenced her.

"Look, Megan. Business is business. We can get any minimum-wage receptionist to come here and answer the telephone and say polite things to our patrons while you're away. I have as much at stake in this charity drive as Yolanda has—maybe more. Now, as Yolanda's partner, I'm ordering you to come with me. We'll fly to the yacht and tour it, then I'll help you write the copy necessary to sell these fishing trips to our patrons, to make them vie for the chance to board *The Golden Dolphin* for a day's outing."

Megan gave in. She had no other choice. Jacques was right. And if he had anything in mind except business he was in for a big surprise. As far as she was concerned this trip was going to be purely for the benefit of the

Yolanda Drive, the Ducruet business interests, and the scholarship fund.

"Get dressed," Jacques said.

"I am dressed."

"You'll need pants, deck shoes," Jacques insisted.

"Then I can't go. Yolanda would never allow me to take time to go shopping."

"No way would I allow you to go shopping either." Jacques picked up the telephone and dialed without looking up the number. While the telephone was ringing he studied Megan's figure.

"Josefina? Jacques Ducruet here. Have you a pair of yachting pants, ladies size eight in bronze? Fine. And a pair of jade green deck shoes, size six narrow? Good. Send them to my hotel suite immediately. Hotel Ducruet, of course."

Megan gritted her teeth, determined not to ask Jacques how he could guess her clothing sizes so accurately. Surely he had known many women intimately. But if he expected her to ask, he didn't let on. He was making another call.

"The usual, Carlos—for two, of course. Deliver immediately to my suite. Hotel Ducruet."

The third call was to the airport. Jacques ordered his plane readied. By the time the phone calls were completed a messenger had arrived with the clothes. Jacques opened the package, inspected the garments, then gave them to Megan.

"Get dressed, please."

Chapter Ten

Megan took the pants and deck shoes to the dressing room, closing the door behind her. Some perverse part of her hoped the pants wouldn't fit, but they clung to her like a second skin, and the shoes also were a perfect fit. She inhaled the new-fabric smell that clung to them. *He's used to shopping for women,* Megan thought. He has a practiced eye where sizes and color are concerned. She found the thought disconcerting as she wondered how many of Yolanda's outfits Jacques had selected.

Megan slipped on a jade green blouse that matched the deck shoes and went back to the living area where Jacques was waiting and smiling. He eyed her approvingly until she felt her face flush. The other package he had ordered had arrived, and Jacques picked it up and headed for the door.

"Let's go, Megan. A receptionist will arrive soon to take over the menial chores. I made the arrangements while you were changing. Bring your notebook, of course."

"Of course." Megan picked up the notebook and some ballpoints and preceeded Jacques from the suite.

Megan inhaled the leather smell of the new upholstery as they rode to the airport in Jacques's Mercedes. When they reached the airstrip, the Cessna was readied and waiting. Diesel exhaust hung in the air and the broiling sunshine heated the airstrip, throwing hot air up into their faces.

Megan noticed a pulse pounding in her fingers as

Jacques took her hand and helped her into the plane. When he slipped across her to get to the pilot's seat, his hips grazed her arm. Her skin prickled with gooseflesh where they had touched. She wondered what it would be like to be able to touch Jacques whenever and wherever she pleased.

"Just don't look down, Megan," Jacques said. "The height won't bother you at all if you look up at the sky."

Megan took Jacques's advice, wondering how many other women had received those same instructions from him. But she was still tense fifteen minutes later when they landed at Contadora. Jacques had buzzed his villa before landing, and in moments José appeared with the Mercedes. He puffed his black cigar as he drove them to a small dock where they boarded a speedboat. With José at the tiller they sliced through the waves to the place where *The Golden Dolphin* floated at anchor.

"How do we get aboard?" Megan asked when José stopped the speedboat and they bobbed on the waves many feet below the yacht's deck. For a moment Megan listened to the waves gently lapping at the hulls of the two boats. This was almost as frightening as the plane ride had been.

"A crewman will lower a boarding ladder," Jacques replied.

Jacques had barely spoken when a man dressed in gold slacks and shirt lowered a gold-painted ladder over the side of the yacht and stood at the deck railing waiting to help them aboard.

"Want me to go first and show you how it's done?" Jacques asked. "Or would you feel safer if you went up first? I'll stay right behind ready to help if you need it."

"I think that would be best."

José grabbed the boarding ladder, pulling the small boat in close to the yacht.

Without waiting for directions from Jacques Megan took hold of the ladder, then placed one foot on a lower rung. The rest was easy, yet she was conscious of the cloth in the new pants pulling across her hips as she climbed. The crewman on deck helped her aboard, and Jacques followed closely behind her.

"Come back in a couple of hours," Jacques called down to José. "We'll be ready to leave by then."

A couple of hours! Megan had thought José would wait on the spot for the few minutes it would take to tour the yacht. She inhaled the salt scent of the sea and wondered what they would do aboard the yacht for two hours. She remembered that Jacques had promised to help her write up the material for the letter and the flyer. Perhaps that was what he had allowed so much time for. Yet she found herself daydreaming of the possibilities. . . . She was glad that the movement of the boat masked her unsteadiness.

The yacht was much larger than it had looked to be from the plane. Megan felt the gentle roll of the craft as they walked the length of the open deck with Jacques pointing out the fishing chairs, the captains' observation booth, the tackle and equipment. The boat was immaculate. And no wonder. Jacques seemed to keep a crew aboard at all times.

"We can travel under sail or under motor," Jacques explained as an onshore breeze cooled them. "I have a crew of excellent Panamanian sailors, but even the best seamen can't move a sailboat if the wind is uncooperative. We will stress in our copy material that we have an alternate source of power."

Megan took hurried notes, then Jacques led her down a companionway to the crew's quarters, the galley, and the captain's quarters. She sniffed a faint odor of canvas and felt the closeness of the warmer air below deck.

"I had no idea a yacht had so much room," Megan murmured as she looked at the bunk beds and chests that lined the bulkhead in the crew's quarters. The captain's quarters were a bit more elegant. A gold spread covered the bed, and a polished walnut desk was built into one bulkhead.

"The yacht sleeps twelve," Jacques said. "Have you ever spent a night at sea, Megan?"

"No, never."

"It's an experience to look forward to. Perhaps . . ."

"I'm sure I'd make a poor sailor," Megan said, speaking up before Jacques could make any more suggestions.

When they reached the galley Jacques laid the package he had carried from the hotel suite onto the table.

"Shall we have lunch, Megan? It's already past noon and I would guess that you are as hungry as I am."

"How thoughtful of you." Megan relaxed a bit, again thinking that perhaps she had misjudged Jacques.

"I believe that employees work better if they're well fed," Jacques said curtly.

Megan sighed. Business first and foremost—that seemed to be his motto. Money made his whole world go around. Money first and women second, she guessed. But what did that matter to her! She had no interest in either his money or his women.

Jacques opened the package to reveal an unsliced loaf of wheat bread, one large ripe avocado, an assortment of salad dressings, and a bottle of wine. With expertise he peeled the avocado and seeded it, mixed the salad dressings to a thick spreading consistency, and sliced the bread.

In a few moments he had made them sandwiches and

poured the sparkling wine to go along with them. The heady aroma made Megan's mouth water. She watched the way Jacques's tanned hands moved as he worked. She could tell he enjoyed the sensual pleasure of touching the bread, the avocado, the wine bottle. It was almost as if he could taste with his fingers.

They lunched on this fare, and the food and wine along with the gentle roll of the yacht made Megan drowsy. She had to fight to keep alert.

"Shall we work on the letter now?" Jacques asked after he had cleared away their lunch things and straightened up the galley. "We can work right here on this table."

"Of course. Where shall we begin?"

"I always like to start things at the beginning." The sardonic smile played about Jacques's lips again.

Megan looked away from him and began writing. "For those who enjoy deep-sea fishing, a day aboard *The Golden Dolphin* . . ."

"Make that a day aboard Jacques Ducruet's *Golden Dolphin*," Jacques said.

Megan made the change, thinking that Jacques was like Yolanda when it came to seeking the limelight. But perhaps advertising a business was several cuts above advertising oneself personally.

They worked steadily for the next hour with Megan writing the rough draft and Jacques adding the polishing touches to the wording. When they finished the letter and the flyer Megan felt sure that Yolanda would approve of the copy.

"We make a good team, Megan. I think even Yolanda will approve of our work on this."

Megan looked through a porthole at the rolling sea, again wondering if Jacques could read her mind. How many times had he voiced the exact thoughts she was thinking!

Jacques peered at his watch. "It's time we were getting back to Panama, Megan. I can't give you my whole day."

"I didn't ask for any of your day," Megan reminded him, refusing to let him make her feel in his debt.

"But I trust you didn't find our time together on my yacht unpleasant."

"Of course not. It was most pleasant indeed. I just hope things have gone as smoothly at the Yolanda suite."

"And if they haven't I will assume full responsibility," Jacques assured her. "Shall we go now?"

Megan stood, suddenly reluctant to leave the yacht. Or was it Jacques's company she was reluctant to leave?

"Who is your lover, Megan?"

Megan felt herself flushing. How dare Jacques ask such a personal question! She glared. And he actually seemed to expect an answer.

"What sort of a man would let you spend two weeks away from him in another man's hotel suite? What sort of a man would let you fly around the country when flying scares you so? What sort of a man, Megan?" Jacques eyed the ring on her finger, picking up her hand for a closer inspection of it.

Megan snatched her hand from his but not before she felt the warm throb caused by his touch. "My ring is part of my mystery, Mr. Ducruet. Clearly you are not immune to the charm of mystery, are you?"

"Most assuredly not. You make me wonder about you. In fact sometimes I find myself daydreaming about you, Megan."

Megan said nothing as they left the galley, climbed to the upper deck and walked to the boarding ladder. José was waiting for them and when he saw them approach the deck railing he pulled the speedboat in close to the yacht. As Megan looked down her head began to reel. This was going to be much more difficult than boarding the yacht had been.

"I'll go first, Megan," Jacques said. "That way I can steady you as you come down."

Megan nodded, refusing to let Jacques know how much looking down into the waves frightened her. She watched him descend the ladder, his muscles rippling beneath his thin shirt, his strong tan hands gripping the sides of the ladder. José steadied him as he stepped down into the speedboat, then he turned and called to her.

"Easy does it, Megan."

A yacht crewman stood ready to help Megan, but she couldn't budge. She felt as if her feet were frozen to the deck.

"Throw one leg over the rail, Megan," Jacques called. "Then find the ladder rung by feel. Don't look down. You'll be okay if you keep your head up and your eyes on the sky."

The sky. Yes. That was it. She would look up as she had when she was climbing aboard the yacht. She hadn't panicked then. Megan looked up, eased one leg over the railing and found the ladder rung with her toe. Placing her foot firmly on the rung, she gripped the sides of the ladder with her hands, eased her other leg over the gunwale and began climbing down.

Down. Down. How could it be so far! Then suddenly she felt Jacques's hands around her ankles.

"Keep coming, Meg. You're doing fine."

Meg. He had called her Meg. Nobody called her that. Not even Vance. She stepped down two more rungs and felt Jacques's hands circle her waist.

"Let go of the ladder and I'll lift you down the rest of the way," he ordered.

Megan let go, feeling the warmth and strength of Jacques's hands through her blouse. At last. She was in the boat. Safe. Then suddenly she was shaking uncontrollably and Jacques was pulling her to a seat in the stern next to him.

"Let's go, José," Jacques ordered. "She'll be okay in a few minutes. Let's get underway."

José eased to the wheel of the boat, started the motor, and they pulled away from the yacht. Although she was still trembling Megan tried to push away from Jacques's embrace, but he only held her more tightly. She hated to admit to herself how much she wanted to relax in his embrace.

"Relax, Megan. Trust me. You're safe now."

Jacques's arm around her waist pulled her tightly to him and she smelled the subtle lime scent that traveled with him. Now he was easing her head onto his shoulder, cradling her as if she were a baby. Gently he tilted her head back so that she looked at him. She wanted to push herself away from him, but she couldn't find the strength nor the will.

"Stop shaking, Megan. I don't like to kiss a girl who is shaking. Just hold onto me. I'll take care of you."

Jacques's voice was incredibly gentle. Mentally Megan pushed him away, but physically she stayed in his arms.

"I promised you a kiss, didn't I? And I never go back on a promise."

Now Megan felt Jacques's lips on her own, first gently, then with a hot firm pressure. Suddenly she was clinging to him, her arms around his neck. She enjoyed his powerful arms encircling her, the firm lips against her own. She felt her body press against his as her whole being responded to the demands his body was making.

When Jacques pulled away from her Megan felt bereft.

"There, there, Megan. You're okay now, aren't you? I hate to think that the descent from the yacht frightened you so badly."

Although Megan wanted to fling herself into Jacques's arms again, to feel his lips against hers once more, she found her poise and dignity and held herself aloof.

"I'm sorry I made such a scene before your crew, Jacques. If you'll forgive me I'll see that it doesn't happen again."

That sardonic smile again! How dare this man play games! That kiss! He had wanted her as much as she had wanted him, yet now he was acting as if they were strangers. Megan was furious with herself. What had she expected? Jacques Ducruet was a smooth operator. Taking ladies to his yacht was just one of his techniques. He played on a woman's fear, her vulnerability, teasing her. Then when she wanted him, he pulled away.

Was this the way Jacques treated Yolanda? Megan wondered. The fact that she would really never know tantalized her. For one woman could never know for sure what a man did with another woman, could she?

Megan ignored the spray that misted against her cheeks as the speedboat cut through the water toward the dock. Once in the Mercedes she sat as far from Jacques as she could while José drove them back to the plane. She gritted her teeth and vowed to show no fear on the flight back to Panama.

"I'll take a taxi back to the hotel," Megan said coolly as they emerged from the airport terminal. "I'm sure you have better things to do with the remainder of your afternoon than to see me back to the suite."

"I never allow my ladies to return home unescorted," Jacques said. He linked his arm through hers and led her to his car.

Megan was still under the spell of their kiss. Although Jacques was merely walking at her side, she could still feel him leaning toward her, protecting her, comforting her, holding her in the circle of his arm as he had done in the speedboat. She couldn't decide whether to be sorry or relieved when he left her at the door to the Yolanda suite. But she soon decided on relieved. She could not afford to fall in love with this playboy. He was a playboy, wasn't he? She wished she knew for sure.

At any rate she could not risk being hurt emotionally again. And her pride in her work along with her desire to repay her grandmother for her schooling strengthened her determination to keep free of all emotional ties, free of all romantic situations that might hurt her.

Once inside the suite Megan dismissed the hired receptionist and flung herself across Jacques's bed sobbing with frustration.

Chapter Eleven

For the next few days Megan and Yolanda worked together, talking with patrons of the Yolanda Drive, selling them on the idea of a Ducruet plane trip to San Blas, a day of deep-sea fishing, an evening at the Ducruet villa on Contadora. It pleased Megan to see the scholarship fund grow.

During these days Megan saw nothing of Jacques and

it bothered her when she was truthful to herself and admitted that she missed him. But how foolish. She was sure he never even thought of her. Many things confirmed this belief.

One morning when she was having pancakes and eggs alone in the hotel's Early Bird room she couldn't help overhearing three ladies at the next table as they visited over their morning coffee.

"Jacques Ducruet is going to get caught one of these days," the first woman said. "Ria de Lopez knows what she wants and I think Ria wants Jacques."

"Ria de Lopez, the cattle heiress?" another woman asked.

"I thought he was after Yolanda Delgado."

Megan could imagine the first woman nodding her head knowingly.

"Delgado is after him, but the de Lopez millions are there for the taking," a third voice said. "Of course Ria goes along with them. Not too bad a deal at that, but I never thought Ria was Jacques Ducruet's type."

Megan felt guilty at eavesdropping, but she couldn't help herself. The conversation fascinated her but at the same time it made her furious. Why did she care who Jacques's ladies were?

"And just what is Jacques Ducruet's type?" the first woman asked with a laugh. "A lot of women in Panama would like to know the answer to that one. I've seen him escorting blondes, brunettes, carrot-tops. I think he's satisfied as long as heads turn when he enters a room. Why, at El Panama the other night . . ."

Megan could stand no more. She motioned to the waiter for her check and left the dining room. Buying a paper at the lobby desk, she carried it to her room and settled down on her balcony to read until Yolanda got up.

After scanning the front-page headlines and the

ready-to-wear ads she turned to Rory Pardo's *About Town* column. Jacques's name leaped out at her as clearly as if it had been set in bold type. She read the words half aloud.

"And who was the lady on Jacques Ducruet's arm at the Taboga Weekender? Rumors fly that she is an actress from Mexico. Whoever she is she upstaged all the other ladies present. How about an introduction, Jacques?"

Megan threw the paper down in disgust. What did she care who Jacques escorted to his fancy parties! She went to her desk, glancing at her watch just as Yolanda emerged from her mirrored room. Today Yolanda wore a shocking pink jumpsuit made from a jersey fabric that clung to every curve. Her raven hair was in a French roll secured with two golden combs and her sandals were a combination of pink and gold. Something about her reminded Megan of a sleek pampered cat. Or was it a lioness?

"Ahha, Megan. Already you are waiting for me and we have so much to do. My tardiness is a crime. Jacques told me we were staying out too late, but I love to see the dawn from the ruins of the Old City. So picturesque. So romantic—and I am a romantic at heart. You must know that by now, don't you? But come! Let's get on with the work of the day, this important day for the Yolanda Drive."

Megan's hand shook as she poured Yolanda a cup of coffee, then poured another cup for herself. She couldn't afford to allow herself to fall in love with Jacques Ducruet. She couldn't base love on one kiss even though it hadn't exactly been a fleeting kiss. Vance had taught her once how painful a broken heart could be. She certainly wasn't ready for a repeat of that experience. But she couldn't help wondering which of his lady friends Jacques liked the most. Was he truly in love with one of them? Yolanda? Yolanda would like for the world to believe that was the case, but Megan wondered. What about Ria? The Mexican actress?

"Megan, are you hearing what I am saying to you?"

Yolanda's voice snapped Megan from her thoughts about Jacques and his women. "I'm sorry, Yolanda. My mind wandered for a moment. But of course I'm listening to you. You were saying something about . . ."

"In just a few minutes we are due at the airport . . . ten o'clock. Jacques's plane will be there. He will call for us presently. Is that the . . . costume . . . you are planning to wear for the flight to San Blas?"

Megan glanced down at her prim skirt and blouse. "I thought it would be all right, but if you think . . ."

"Better to wear pants," Yolanda said. "Wear the ones Jacques bought you for the yacht tour. They are just the thing."

Megan forced herself to show no emotion when she heard the subtly superior tone of Yolanda's voice. So Jacques had told Yolanda about their visit to the yacht, about the clothes! It had meant nothing more to him than a business trip. She forced herself to meet Yolanda's gaze. In the back of her mind she felt sure Jacques had not told Yolanda about their kiss.

"Of course I'll change into the pants if you think that would be suitable. It'll only take me a moment." Megan hurried from her desk to the dressing room, and Yolanda followed her before she could close the door. With Yolanda watching her every move, Megan quickly slipped from her skirt and blouse. She felt exposed and vulnerable as Yolanda openly appraised her figure.

Moving quickly she tugged on the bronze-colored pants and added the jade green blouse. The pants were her color. Jacques knew how to dress a woman. Shoes? She could hardly wear the deck shoes on so elegant an occasion. No. She would wear heels. They gave her outfit a dressier appearance. As she bent over to pick up the heels Yolanda walked behind her, giving a throaty laugh.

"Jacques said the pants were a nice fit," Yolanda said. "As always he was right. We want you to look your best, of course." Yolanda studied Megan's shoes. "Do you think you'll be comfortable in such a high heel?"

Megan looked Yolanda in the eye. "I'm sure I'll be perfectly comfortable, Yolanda. But thank you for your concern. Sometimes it is hard to know what to wear."

"Don't forget your notebook," Yolanda reminded. "You may need it."

"I have it right here." Megan patted her shoulder purse as they left the dressing room. "We have six passengers going to San Blas this morning, right?"

"Six. Six thousand dollars for the Yolanda Drive. And we will fly back for a second group while the first group is having lunch at Porvenir. Another six thou. It's easy to raise money when one knows how."

The telephone rang and Megan picked it up. "Yolanda headquarters. May I help you?"

"Mr. Ducruet is waiting for Miss Delgado and Miss Taylor," a heavily accented voice replied.

"Tell Mr. Ducruet that Miss Delgado and Miss Taylor will be right down." Megan replaced the receiver and turned to Yolanda. "Shall we go? Jacques is waiting."

Yolanda nodded, checked her appearance in a mirror one last time, then swept from the suite. Megan followed her. Downstairs Yolanda managed to keep two paces ahead as they left the elevator and walked toward Jacques who was waiting at the desk. This morning he wore a cream-colored shirt and tan slacks that accented his slim waist and hips. Megan kept her distance, not wanting to smell the lime scent that tantalized her so.

"I thought you might have come up to the suite and have coffee with me before we faced the day." Yolanda pouted prettily, looking up at Jacques through her sooty lashes. "I really needed a pick-me-up after last night."

Jacques pointed to his watch. "We've no time for dallying, Yolanda. Come on. We're going to be late."

"But my dear, I planned for us to be a little late. People expect to wait for Yolanda Delgado. It would spoil my image to be on time."

"People may be willing to wait for you, but airline take-off schedules are a different matter. Come on. Let's get going. Are you ready, Megan?"

For the first time that morning Jacques seemed to notice Megan and she nodded curtly. "I'm ready."

"You look very nice this morning." Jacques grinned. "I like women in pants."

You like women, period, Megan thought. She slipped into the back seat of the Mercedes, then Yolanda sat in front beside Jacques. It seemed that the car reeked of gardenia scent. Yolanda had left her mark. Surely the scent lingered from last night. Megan watched the way Jacques's strong hands guided the car through the heavy traffic that clogged the highway to the airport. Efficient. That was what Jacques was. Efficient. Efficient at many things. Megan could not help remembering their kiss aboard the speedboat.

"I can hardly wait for the Contadora gala," Yolanda said as they rode along. "We could surprise everyone, Jacques. We could turn the gala into something really great, something Panama would long remember."

"I don't know what you mean, Yolanda." Jacques kept his gaze on the road. "It already is something great and something memorable. We have fifty couples signed up at the stupendous price of a thousand dollars per couple."

Yolanda gazed up at him. "We could give them even more for their money than an evening of dining and dancing. I hope you will think about it, Jacques."

Megan sat very still. What could Yolanda be hinting at except an announcement of their engagement! Suddenly she felt cold and very small. Were Jacques and Yolanda that serious about each other? Was Jacques in love with Yolanda? It had bothered her to hear rumors about Jacques and to read his name in the gossip columns. But at least she had felt there was safety in numbers. He had not settled for any one woman . . . yet. But Yolanda seemed to be pushing for just that. A declaration of his love for her to be made in public.

Megan's mouth was so dry she could hardly swallow and she hated the stale coffee taste that coated her tongue. What difference did Jacques's relationship to Yolanda make to her? Jacques didn't even know she existed in any capacity other than efficient secretary.

I'm in love, Megan thought. The admission made her weak. *I'm in love again with a man who doesn't love me.* She straightened in the seat. *But this time the man will never know my feelings. I'll not wear my heart on my sleeve for everyone to see and to laugh at. At the end of these two weeks I'll never see Jacques Ducruet again. I'll have Yolanda's recommendation for another job and I'll devote my full time and talent to my career in the business world.*

"Do you plan to remain in the car, Megan?"

Megan flushed as she realized Jacques was talking to her. While she had been dreaming he had parked the Mercedes. Yolanda had gotten out, and now Jacques was holding the door for her, stooping slightly to peer inside. Megan eased from the back seat, refusing to answer Jacques's question or to respond to the teasing glance he gave her. She followed him and Yolanda into the terminal building. Someone had spilled a bottle of grape pop and the grape scent overpowered the smoke odor that hung in the room.

Now Yolanda took over. She climbed on a chair, towering over the rest of the people waiting for flights and boarding passes. "The Yolanda flight to San Blas is ready for departure."

At the sound of Yolanda's throaty voice everyone stopped talking and stared. Yolanda basked in the attention.

"Please follow our pilot, Jacques Ducruet, out to the plane. In just thirty minutes you will find yourselves transported to a different world, a land where time has stood still for centuries. Come now, let us go."

Jacques offered his hand to help Yolanda down from the chair, and Megan noticed the way Yolanda held onto that hand all the way out to the plane. One by one Jacques helped the passengers board the Cessna. Again Megan sat in the seat directly behind Jacques with Yolanda at his side.

Megan refrained from looking down as the plane took off and gained altitude. She tried to concentrate on the chatter of the six ladies seated behind her. As long as she looked straight ahead into blue sky she felt no fear of the great height. Jacques's voice helped put her at ease as he spoke into a microphone and gave the patrons a brief history of the San Blas islands and the Cuna Indians.

"The islands are only large enough for the thatch-roofed huts you will see on them. Some of the men make a living by traveling in dugout canoes to the mainland where they tend coconut groves, selling the coconuts as a cash crop. The women of the islands do the housekeeping chores. This sometimes includes boating to a mainland river to replenish the household supply of fresh water. In their free time the women appliqué the colorful molas you see for sale in the posh shops in Panama."

Now Yolanda interrupted, taking the microphone from Jacques. "Today, ladies, you will be able to purchase molas directly from these creative artists. It all has been arranged by Yolanda Delgado."

Jacques leaned toward Yolanda. "Shall I warn them about taking pictures? We don't want any trouble, or any unfortunate misunderstandings."

"It won't be necessary to warn them," Yolanda replied softly. "It's true that the natives expect to be paid for posing for pictures. But I've arranged to pay a flat fee that will cover any photos the guests want to take."

"Good thinking." Jacques smiled at Yolanda in a way that Megan couldn't interpret. Was he in love with her?

Their touchdown on the grassy airstrip at Porvenir was smooth. Jacques alighted first and helped the passengers out. Native women peeked at them from their thatched huts while a jeans-clad spokesman for the Cunas greeted Yolanda and made arrangements for dugout boat tours to the outlying islands and a return to Porvenir for a late lunch. Men lolling in hammocks in a thatched shack ignored the newcomers.

Yolanda basked in the attention of the charity patrons, leading them down to the tiny dock where a yellow-painted dugout and a native guide waited.

"Do you want to visit the out-islands?" Jacques asked Megan.

"I think I'll just wait here. I've visited the islands before. I could do with some relaxing."

"Mind if I relax with you?"

"As you choose." Megan bought a bottle of cola from a native in the open-air dining pavilion and sat down at a table overlooking the dock and the sea. She watched a bright-eyed parrot perched in a seagrape tree until Jacques joined her. He said nothing and in moments Megan began to fidget as the silence between them became electric.

"I can't imagine these people being content to live out their lives in such isolation," Megan said. "What do they have to look forward to?"

"What does anyone have to look forward to?" Jacques asked. "Life, death, taxes. At least the Cunas probably don't have very high taxes. And the isolation could be very nice—depending on whom you are isolated with, of course."

"Of course." Megan ignored the suggestiveness in Jacques's tone and gazed out at the blue-green water where two men floated in a small canoe. "What are those fellows doing, Jacques? They don't seem to be fishing."

"They're diving for lobster. At least I think that's what they're doing. Sometimes the men dredge rock from the sea, rock and sand and gravel, haul it out to a marked site, and dump it. They create new islands for their people in that manner, so I've been told."

"That must take them forever."

"So?" Jacques laughed. "As far as I can see they're on no rigid time schedule."

Megan smiled in spite of herself. "No. I suppose not. And eventually a new island will give them more living space." Megan watched two gulls flying so close together they looked like one bird with four wings. It was pleasant to have time to relax and just sit and enjoy.

"Shall we tour the island on foot?" Jacques asked

when they finished their drinks. "I like to walk and nobody will object, I'm sure."

Megan rose, telling herself that she was only going with Jacques because there was nothing else to do. But her heart thumped a bit faster. As they left the pavilion she stopped to admire the mola wall hangings. Then they paused in the seagrape where three Cuna women sat in the shade, displaying molas, shell necklaces, and wood carvings. Megan admired a necklace and Jacques immediately purchased it for her.

"Jewels from the sea," he said, lowering the necklace over her head and draping it around her neck.

Megan vowed to admire nothing more on the island. She didn't intend to accept any more gifts from Jacques Ducruet no matter how inexpensive.

"Look, Jacques. Look at that hut on our left. There's a woman hiding behind it and peeking at us."

Jacques looked casually, then smiled at Megan. "She's an albino. The Cunas suffer from a high rate of albinoism, and the albinos hate to be seen by visitors. In the old days an albino baby was put to death at birth. Now the Cunas let the albinos live, but they still live the life of an outcast."

"How terrible for them." Megan shuddered and looked away from the hut where the woman was still hiding. They walked on, pausing to watch a native boy open a coconut with a machete, drink the water, then cut the white meat into chunks which he tossed into a straw basket.

Megan gasped as a green and gold parrot perched on her shoulder. Jacques held out his finger and the bird stepped onto it, pecked at the diamond in his ring, then flew back to its wooden perch near the pavilion.

"An island pet, no doubt," Megan said. "It startled me. Parrots can be mean, I've heard."

They strolled down to the dock where a fisherman wearing cutoffs and a straw hat was mending his nets and where two naked boys were diving for starfish.

"They'll try to sell those to Yolanda's group when the dugout returns," Jacques said. "And the ladies will buy, all the while getting an eyeful and wishing the boys were a bit older."

"Jacques!" Megan laughed although she tried not to.

Under any other circumstances Megan would have enjoyed the sea and the sun and the slow pace of the day, but with Jacques at her side she felt vulnerable and on guard. Was this the same man who had kissed her so passionately aboard the speedboat at Contadora? What sort of a man could turn his feelings on and off with such precision? She could have been walking with a stranger. Perhaps she *was* walking with a stranger. She felt a separation between them that she couldn't describe.

Chapter Twelve

As soon as Yolanda and the patrons returned to the pavilion Yolanda saw that lunch was served, then she and Megan and Jacques flew back to Panama to pick up the second tour group. While Yolanda accompanied the second group on its tour of the out-islands Jacques and Megan accompanied the first group home, then returned to San Blas for the second group.

That night in her room Megan felt bone tired, but she also fought restlessness. Perhaps because she had spent the day on the sunswept beach of the quiet uncrowded island she felt cooped up in the hotel suite that night. It was almost ten o'clock when she decided to go out for a walk. Nobody would be calling at this hour and as long as she walked alone she wouldn't be breaking any of Yolanda's rules.

Megan left the hotel by the front door and strolled down the hill toward the bridge that crossed the bay. The scent of jasmine wafted around her in the soft night and she watched a fluff of clouds scud across the starlit sky. She loved Panama at this season. No rain. Warm balmy nights. Paradise. She listened to the breeze rustle the palm fronds at the edge of the sidewalk.

As she passed through a wooded area Megan thought she heard footsteps behind her. Instinctively she held her purse more tightly. Panama had a low crime rate, especially in the better sections of the city, but even so, purse-snatching was a favorite hobby of some of the young men from the slums.

The footsteps were coming closer. Suddenly Megan realized she had been foolish to venture to this isolated spot alone. Turning, she was heading back toward the hotel when a stocky youth blocked her way on the sidewalk. Megan stepped into the street, but the boy followed, speaking to her softly in Spanish. Megan smelled the stench of decaying matter left on the bay shore by the outgoing tide mingling with the sweetish odor of the boy's cigarette.

Her purse. He wanted her purse. Her money. Shaking with fear and anger Megan slipped the purse from her shoulder and was about to hand it to the accoster when she heard more footsteps. Was she going to be attacked? She wanted to run, but she couldn't lift her feet.

"Váyase!"

"Jacques!" Megan exclaimed, feeling her pulse pound in her throat. "Oh, Jacques! I'm so glad you came along."

"Váyase!" Jacques shouted at the boy a second time, doubled his fist and took a threatening step toward him. The boy backed off slowly at first, his eyes blazing like those of a cornered lynx. Then he turned and ran across the street, disappearing into a park thick with tropical growth.

"Stupid!" Jacques said, his voice steely calm. "How could you be so stupid as to go out walking alone at night, Megan? No decent woman in this city would pull such a stunt."

Megan bristled at being called stupid, but she kept her voice just as steely as Jacques's. "I made a mistake. I felt hemmed in up in the suite and I wanted some fresh air. Gram and I often take a late-night turn around the block in the Canal Zone."

"That's a completely different situation. You can do some things in the zone that you can't do in the city proper."

"Thank you for coming to my rescue," Megan said. Now she was shaking as she realized the danger she had been in.

"You could have been killed."

"I know." She fought to keep her voice steady. "I said thank you and I meant it. I'll say it again. Thank you for rescuing me. How did you happen to be out walking?"

"I was following you."

"Jacques! Did Yolanda ask you to do that? Did she think I was out to meet . . . someone?"

"Don't misunderstand. Yolanda had nothing to do with it. I saw you leave the hotel alone and I knew it was a stupid thing for you to do, so I followed you.

Yolanda can't handle this charity drive without efficient help. If anything happened to you I know the charity drive would be jeopardized and my interests along with it. So I followed you. And it's a good thing for you that I did. A good thing for everyone."

Megan felt her nails dig into her palms. "It certainly is a good thing you followed me, Mr. Ducruet. I should have known that you had no thought for my personal safety, only concern for your precious charity drive, your all-important advertising of the Ducruet Enterprises. If I had been raped and murdered it wouldn't have mattered to you as long as the charity drive was not inconvenienced." Megan turned and started back toward the hotel, but before she had taken two steps Jacques grabbed her wrist, stopping her.

"You little spitfire. You planned this whole scene, didn't you? You probably paid that boy to stage a phony purse-snatching. It's just another of your not-so-subtle ways of throwing yourself at me."

Megan gasped and felt her whole being coil in anger. "Throwing myself at you! How dare you insinuate such a thing. I'm wearing an engagement ring, you know. I care nothing for you or any other man."

"You lie, Megan Taylor. You lie."

Jacques pulled Megan toward him, encircled her with his arms and kissed her as he had kissed her once before, first gently pressing his mouth to hers, then increasing the pressure, the demand. For a moment Megan refused to respond to his kiss, then as her lips parted, warmth flooded her body and she kissed him passionately. Pulling her lips from his she kissed his cheeks, his throat.

But suddenly Jacques withdrew and held her at arm's length. It astonished her to find she was panting for breath.

"Ah, and you say you have no feeling for me. You lie, Megan. You are wearing a phony engagement ring, aren't you? I can't for the life of me guess why. But you don't fool me; I know you love no other man. If the ring is not phony, then I feel sorry for the fool it belongs to."

"You're wrong," Megan declared. "I care nothing for you. I am an engaged woman. Save your kisses for Yolanda and your heiress and your actress from across the border. I want no part of you."

Megan expected an angry retort from Jacques, but instead she found him grinning down at her as if he enjoyed her discomfort. She wanted to stamp her foot and scream and throw a tantrum, but her business school poise saved her from that embarrassment. Hadn't she been through enough for one day!

Jacques tilted his head provocatively as he looked down at her. "If you really don't care for me I want you to prove it."

"I am trying to prove it. I am telling you in plain language that I do not care for you."

"Telling and showing are two different things. I want you to show me that you don't care."

"Right. I will show you. I'll walk back to the hotel without so much as another glance at you. You will never again find me so vulnerable as I was tonight."

Megan turned to leave Jacques and return to the hotel, but he seized her hand and stood in front of her, blocking her exit.

"Say you're in love with me, Megan. Admit your true feelings and let's stop all this nonsense. No girl could kiss a man the way you kissed me without being deeply attracted to that man."

"That's not true."

"I could feel your heart pounding, Megan. I could

feel your body melt into mine in a way that said you want me. Body language speaks more loudly than words."

"You want to hear me say I love you, don't you? You want to add me to your long list of pining ladies? Not on your life!" Megan tried to jerk free, but Jacques kept a firm grip on her hand.

"What is the difference in letting your body say you love me and saying you love me with words?"

"Kisses are easily misunderstood," Megan said, struggling for control. Jerking free of Jacques's grip, she started walking haughtily toward the hotel. Jacques strode at her side, making no attempt to stop her.

"Kisses are misunderstood, are they?"

Megan refused to reply, and Jacques followed her to the hotel, across the lobby, stopping her hand as she reached to press the elevator button. "I think I understood your kiss well enough, Megan. And I believe I understand your unspoken words. You love me. I think you set up a phony distress situation as a means of getting my attention."

Megan was so angry and confused that she didn't dare risk a reply. She pushed the elevator button, stepped inside the cage and waited for the door to close. She knew that the next few days would be difficult, but she could be as stubborn as Jacques. She would never let him know how much she cared for him. No matter what, Jacques Ducruet would always remember Megan Taylor as the woman who didn't fall for his wealth, his fast line, or his kisses.

Chapter Thirteen

Megan slept poorly that night, tossing and turning, listening to the traffic noises drifting from the highway. Once she rose, slipped a cotton robe over her body and stepped onto her balcony. The damp night air was heavy with the scent of salt and jasmine. She was leaning with her forearms on the balcony railing when voices drifted up to her.

Looking down far below she saw Yolanda and Jacques. The hotel pool was closed at that hour and nobody else was about.

"Come swim with me, Jacques." Yolanda loosened the sash on her champagne-colored robe, letting it fall open. Moonlight gleamed on her flawless skin. Megan noticed that no tan line marked the boundaries of a bikini and she knew that Yolanda must always sunbathe in the nude. Where? She could only wonder.

"It's against rules to swim at night." Jacques said the words lightly at the same time he let his white robe fall onto a beach chair.

"Surely the owner of the hotel can change the rules to suit his desires." Yolanda looked up at him provocatively and he eased her robe from her body, tossing it down with his own.

For a moment Jacques and Yolanda reminded Megan of alabaster statues. They stood motionless, devouring each other with their eyes. Megan watched fascinated as Yolanda reached to put her arms around Jacques's neck. As she reached up Jacques stepped sideways and

made a graceful dive into the pool. He surfaced halfway
across the deep end and Megan watched the way the
moonlight played on his skin. She felt weak with desire
for Jacques; at the same time hot anger at Yolanda's
brazenness flooded her.

"Wait for me, Jacques." Yolanda dove into the pool,
swimming like an elegant seal to where Jacques was
treading water.

"I'm waiting, my dear."

Yolanda caught Jacques's hair in her right hand,
tilting his head back until the moonlight shone full on
his face. Pressing her body to his, her lips parted as she
kissed him before they gradually disappeared beneath
the surface.

"Hussy!" Megan half whispered. Then she could
bear to watch no more. She wanted to blame the whole
scene on Yolanda, yet she knew she was kidding
herself. It was not Yolanda who had undressed Jacques.
True, he had avoided her first come-on kiss, but Megan
had watched his hands play against Yolanda's skin as
they submerged together.

What would they do when they finished swimming?
Megan tried not to think about it. She tried to sleep,
but sleep didn't come until she heard Yolanda enter the
suite a little before dawn.

The next morning Megan dressed carefully. She
applied light makeup to the dark shadows under her
eyes and she put on bright lipstick, smudging a dab of it
onto her cheekbones and rubbing it in to try to bring
her face alive. When she stepped to her desk, Yolanda
spoke first.

"You poor dear." Yolanda looked at Megan with a
studied gaze. "I understand from Jacques that you had
a frightful experience last night."

Megan hesitated before answering. Last night had

been absolutely filled with terrible experiences. To see the man she loved bathing nude with another woman was much more painful than the attempted purse-snatching, but she guessed Yolanda was referring to the attempted theft.

"Yes, Yolanda. I was quite frightened. It was lucky that Jacques appeared on the scene to offer help."

"Very lucky indeed." Yolanda purred the words. "He told me *all* about it later. He was really quite the hero, wasn't he?"

Megan felt herself flushing. What was Yolanda trying to say to her? Was she being sarcastic? Did she think that Megan had staged the purse-snatching to attract Jacques? Megan could hardly stop the questions that filled her mind.

"I think I can do without you, Megan."

Megan gasped. So Jacques had told all. And now she was being fired. She felt something inside her curl up and die.

"Don't look so striken, my dear." Yolanda laughed. "Usually I go to Contadora personally to make arrangements for any gala to be held there. But you've done such a good job of organizing this work that I can do without you here in the suite for a day or two. I've made a reservation for you on the 10:00 A.M. flight to Contadora. I've written out instructions. You can discuss the details with José and Juanita."

Megan breathed again, but even as she relaxed she knew Yolanda had chosen her words with care, chosen them to achieve a desired effect. "You mean you're turning all the plans for the gala over to me?"

"That's right." Yolanda smiled and held a manila envelope toward Megan. "The instructions are in here. You discuss them with the servants. Make plans for hiring extra help. Make out a list of groceries and liquors that will be needed. I'll order them here and send them over on a commercial flight later. Do you have any questions?"

Megan opened the envelope and glanced over the instructions Yolanda had drawn up. "No, Yolanda. I can't think of any questions right now. You seem to have thought of everything."

"Call me here at the suite if you run into any problems. Take an overnight bag. You'll stay the night. Then Jacques and I will fly over and discuss final arrangements. Hurry now. I've called for a taxi to take you to the airport."

Megan packed her overnight things and an extra work outfit, stuffed the manila envelope of instructions into her purse, and hurried to the hotel lobby where the taxi driver was waiting for her. It wasn't until she was aboard the plane and flying over the sea that she realized Yolanda was sending her to Contadora to get rid of her, to get her away from Jacques's presence. The thought frightened her. She didn't want Yolanda to feel she was a threat.

"Going to Contadora suits me just fine," Megan muttered to herself. "It's safer this way. If I'm not near him I'm not in danger of revealing my feelings for him."

"What did you say, ma'am?" the stewardess asked, bending toward her.

"Nothing." Megan blushed at having been caught talking to herself. "Nothing at all, miss. I was just thinking out loud."

The stewardess smiled and passed on down the narrow aisle.

When the plane touched down on the Contadora airstrip Megan waited in her seat until the rest of the passengers had disembarked. Limousines and open-air jeeps from the hotel picked up passengers and luggage. It was a moment before she spotted José and the Mercedes. She waved, and José ground out his black cigar under his heel, slid from the car, and hurried toward her.

"*Buenos días,* Señorita. You have luggage?"

"Just an overnight case, José." Megan smiled at José as he picked up her case. "What a beautiful day! I hope Juanita is expecting me."

José grinned and bowed as he took her case. "This time she has been informed. She has a room ready and waiting for your arrival." José slipped the overnight case in the back seat and motioned Megan to sit up front with him. As usual the Mercedes reeked of stale smoke.

Once Megan was settled she gazed across the vast expanse of the sea.

"The water never looks the same twice does it?" she asked. "Lime green. Cobalt blue. Chartreuse."

"The sea is ever changing," José answered. "Like a woman."

Like a woman . . . Megan thought . . . *perhaps the old saying should be changed to "like a man."* She sighed. But back to business. She touched her purse reassuringly. Yes, the manila envelope with Yolanda's instructions was still there. . . .

José drove slowly over the winding road. Sometimes they had a clear view of the sea and at other times they seemed surrounded by scrub palm thickets. Megan wondered who lived in all the secluded cottages she saw tucked in hidden coves and almost hidden by palms and seagrape. Lovers? Vacationers? Retired folk?

She was about to ask José about the people of the island when he spoke. "Here we are, Miss Megan." He slowed the Mercedes, driving it into a carport where a latticework trellis covered with philodendron shaded it from the sun. "Juanita has prepared brunch."

"It seems that I always arrive in time to eat," Megan said, smiling. "I really don't plan it that way."

José helped Megan from the car. "We know. Juanita and I know that Miss Yolanda makes the plans. But brunch is no trouble. Come. Follow me."

Megan followed José into the brown villa. Sun shining through the vines on the lattice entryway dappled the teakwood floor, and Megan removed her sunglasses in order to see the true colors of her surroundings. A salmon-colored bird-of-paradise plant bloomed in one corner, and a fan-shaped arrangement of palm fronds and golden hibiscus blossoms accented a teakwood coffee table.

"I'll take you to the patio," José said. "Then I'll put your bag in your room. Juanita will serve brunch soon."

"Perhaps we can go over some of Yolanda's plans while we eat," Megan suggested.

"There is no hurry," José said. "Juanita and I have worked on this gala many times. It is an old thing to us and we are comfortable with it. The party never changes from year to year, only the people are different."

José led Megan to the bamboo table, raised the yellow umbrella to shade her. "Make yourself comfortable. I'll be back in a few minutes."

Megan sat down and gazed across the sea. Gulls wheeled and dived and screamed like angry children. Frigate birds looked like black kites as they floated on updrafts, seldom moving their wings. She inhaled the sweet salt scent of the water and welcomed the feel of the cool breeze against her warm cheeks.

So the gala didn't change from year to year. José and

Juanita knew what to do. . . . Clearly, Yolanda knew what to do too—to get Megan as far away from Jacques as possible. Why hadn't Yolanda fired her? Megan mulled that question over in her mind, but she reached no simple answer. Pride? Need? Who could say?

"Maybe she felt she'd lose face if she fired me," Megan murmured.

"Did you call miss?" Juanita had arrived so silently that Megan jumped at the sound of her voice.

"I was just talking to myself," Megan admitted, blushing. "It's a bad habit I seem to have developed lately."

Juanita smiled. "Sometimes I find that working for Miss Yolanda makes one talk to oneself."

Megan grinned, liking Juanita immediately. "I think we understand each other, Juanita."

Juanita set a pitcher of orange juice and three glasses on the table and returned to the kitchen for a bamboo teacart that held the rest of the brunch. Today Juanita seemed relaxed and unhurried. She wore a peach-colored skirt topped with a sleeveless shell. A silver necklace and earrings gleamed against her bronze skin and her barefoot sandals slapped against the flagstones of the patio.

"I didn't know I was hungry until I smelled that bacon and eggs, Juanita. And that coffee! I didn't know it could smell so delicious."

Juanita served the brunch, but they waited until José joined then before they began eating. At first Megan thought Juanita had prepared a great surplus of food, but as José began to eat, she realized that Juanita had not overdone it. After twenty minutes all the fruit, eggs, and bacon had disappeared and only a few slices of cinnamon toast remained on the plate.

As they lingered over coffee, Megan pulled the manila envelope from her purse. "Here are our instructions. Would you like to go over them with me now?"

Juanita began clearing the table as if she were completely uninterested. "Why do we not give you a tour of the villa first? You have seen little of it so far. The instructions will mean more to you after you see where the party will be held."

"That sounds like a good idea," Megan said. "I supposed the party would be held right here on this patio overlooking the cove. I can hardly imagine a nicer spot. A little moonlight. A soft breeze. Some romantic music. What more is needed?"

José stood and began stacking their dishes on the tea cart. "Part of the guests will be out here, Miss Megan. But you must see the inside of the villa too. That is where the orchestra will set up. And there will be a large buffet table near the dance floor."

"No dancing on the patio?" Megan asked.

"The stones are quite uneven," Juanita replied. "Do come inside and look around."

Megan followed José and Juanita inside the villa. To the left of the entry a spiral stairway rose like a giant corkscrew to the second floor. Megan felt a cool draft flow down the opening.

"Perhaps you would like to freshen up," Juanita invited. "Come, I'll show you your room while José wheels the teacart to the kitchen."

Megan followed Juanita up the polished teakwood steps to the second floor. Here suites of bedrooms opened off a hallway that formed a balcony on one side from which one could look down onto a ballroom below. Juanita led the way into a room decorated in shades of pale green and gold.

"Mr. Jacques has requested that you have this suite,"

Juanita said. She looked Megan over carefully. "He has chosen well. The colors suit you."

"And does Jacques always match his rooms to his ladies-in-residence?" Megan felt herself blushing.

"Quite frequently." Juanita grinned at Megan. "I'll unpack for you while you freshen up. Then I'll show you the other rooms."

Megan retired to the spacious mirrored bathroom where she repaired her makeup and combed her hair. She ran cool water over her wrists, feeling her whole body relax and grow more comfortable. She wished she could kick her shoes off and feel the cool tiles beneath her bare feet, but she knew she would have to wait for that luxury.

Once again she joined Juanita in the bedroom. The bed was made up with satin sheets only, and the windows were curtained in a matching fabric with the same hibiscus design. A thatched matting on the floors made the room feel cool and spacious. In spite of the luxurious surroundings Megan couldn't help wondering what other women had spent nights here. Then she noticed the rose. In a crystal bud vase on the bedside table a single rosebud wafted its sweet scent into the room. Jacques's idea? Megan was too shy to ask.

Juanita nodded toward a spacious closet. "I've hung your robe and your extra slacks and blouse on hangers. I found no nightdress, though."

Again Megan felt herself blushing. She hadn't expected someone else to unpack for her. "I must have overlooked it in my haste to catch the plane."

"I'll send one up for you," Juanita said. "I believe we have some green ones on hand."

"Thank you." Megan felt a chill forming in the pit of her stomach. Did Jacques Ducruet supply all his female visitors with nightwear? She lowered her gaze as she felt Juanita staring at her. What did she care how Jacques Ducruet lived! He was of no concern to her. None at all.

"Come," Juanita said. "I'll show you the rest of the bedrooms."

Megan followed with a mixture of reluctance and curiosity. She peeked into a room decorated in hibiscus pink and into another done in sea blues and grays. The walls of a third suite had been covered in lemon-yellow silk, and a fourth suite had been done completely in silver and mirrors. Surely that was the one Yolanda usually occupied. She could imagine Yolanda's voluptuous body stretched out on the shimmering sheet. And did Jacques furnish her with a silver nightgown?

"And this is Señor Jacques's suite." Juanita stood back to let Megan look through the doorway.

Megan gasped. "How n-nice," she murmured. How like him, she thought. The room was done boldly in black and white. White walls and white wicker furniture. Black satin sheets and draperies. Megan could smell the scent of lime that she had come to associate with Jacques. Where was it coming from? How did he manage to have it everywhere about him? For a moment she imagined Jacques's tanned body relaxing against the dark, gleaming satin of the sheets. But it was hard to imagine Jacques in bed alone. How many women had lain on the smooth sheets beside him, caressed and caressing his lean body? She felt herself flushing.

When they were back downstairs Juanita opened the sliding glass ballroom doors. Now Megan heard waves crashing on the shore below. She watched the water froth on the white sand, recede, then swirl up on the beach again.

"You like to swim?" Juanita asked.

"I love to." Megan listened to the roar of the surf.

"You will be free this afternoon," Juanita said. "You must go down to the beach and relax for a while." Then she turned and faced the room. "We set up the buffet table against that wall, Miss Megan. The silver candelabra will be polished for the event. The whole room will have nothing but candlelight."

"That sounds very romantic."

"The musicians are seated in this corner by the sliding doors." Juanita walked to the place. "Marimba, guitar, drums. The dancing goes on until dawn."

Megan inspected the kitchen, then they returned to the outdoor patio. "Perhaps we'd better read over Yolanda's instructions," Megan said. She sat down at the table and pulled the envelope from her purse once more. This time she removed the white sheets and spread them out in front of herself and Juanita.

"You are to hire extra maids and extra kitchen help," Megan said. "Five maids and three cooks."

"And they are to be in formal attire, is that not right?"

"Right. And here is the menu. Crabmeat soufflé. Broccoli and rice casserole topped with mushrooms. Fresh fruit salad with lemon dressing. Relish trays with sour cream dips. Boiled jumbo shrimp with a cold tomato sauce. Clam dip and crackers. Assorted cheese balls and hot and cold cheese dips."

"It's always the same."

"Yolanda wants me to give her your grocery list. She'll fill it in Panama and have it flown over to you."

"As always," Juanita said. "I have the list from last year. It worked out well. We will use the same recipes, the same quantities." Juanita pulled the list from her pocket.

"You're a wonder, Juanita," Megan said. "Isn't there something I can do to help you with all this? I don't feel as if I'm earning my pay."

"Just telephone the grocery list to Yolanda and ask her to get the supplies to me as soon as possible. Today if she can. I'll get my helpers here tomorrow and we'll start preparing the buffet delicacies that can be kept in the refrigerator. Others will have to wait until closer to serving time."

Megan took the grocery list Juanita offered. "I really don't see why Yolanda sent me over here. You have things well in hand. . . . " she said aloud. But her heart already knew the answer to her question.

Chapter Fourteen

"Where may I find a telephone?" Megan asked.

"There is one in your room." Juanita stood. "Now I must go round up my workers. Some have no telephones. I must go to them personally."

"May I help with that?"

"No. You call the list to Yolanda. Then why don't you spend the rest of the afternoon relaxing on the beach?"

"I brought no beach clothes. Really, I came here to work, not to play."

"You'll find beach things in your room. Make yourself at home. The villa is yours. Now if you'll excuse me, I'll be off. José will drive me to talk with the extra maids."

"Of course." Megan waited until Juanita disappeared back inside the villa, then she took the grocery list and climbed the spiral stairs to her room.

Megan used operator assistance to put her call through to the Yolanda suite in Panama. She was nonplussed when Jacques's voice answered the ring, but she kept her voice steady.

"I want to speak to Yolanda, please."

"And who is calling?" Jacques asked.

"Megan Taylor." Megan said her name as if she had not recognized Jacques's voice, and she guessed that he was playing the same game. In an instant Yolanda was on the wire. Megan wondered if she had broken up a tête-à-tête between them. Clearly Yolanda was glad to have her out of the way.

"What is it, Megan?" Yolanda asked. "We are very busy here at headquarters."

"I have Juanita's grocery order," Megan said. "Shall I read it to you? She would like to have the things in her kitchen today if it is possible."

"It is not possible," said Yolanda firmly. "By the time I order the things and they are delivered, there will be no more flights to Contadora."

"Then could you send them over first thing tomorrow morning?" Megan asked. "There are many preparations to be made. Juanita insists on the groceries as soon as possible."

"Tomorrow morning," Yolanda said. "Tell her that is the best I can do."

"All right." Megan sighed and began reading the list. When she finished, Yolanda read it back to her so they could double check the order.

"Good work, Megan. Now, please oversee Juanita carefully. I want this gala to be a stunning success."

"Of course, Yolanda. And when will I be returning to Panama?"

"We'll see. I'll let you know when the time is right. Of course we will need to shop for you for something to wear to the gala. I must think about that. In meantime, help Juanita, will you?"

"Of course." There was a click in Megan's ear. Yolanda had hung up. Megan replaced the receiver and stared into space for a moment or two. She inhaled the scent of the rose and tried not to imagine what Yolanda and Jacques might be doing in the hotel suite. It was certainly none of her business.

After Megan heard José and Juanita leave in the Mercedes she checked in her room for some beachwear. In a top dresser drawer she found a brief bikini that fit her as if it had been ordered for her. She couldn't help preening for a moment before the mirror. Then she paused as a thought hit her. *Had* the bikini been ordered especially for her? Had Jacques ordered it as he had ordered the deck shoes and the yachting pants?

Grabbing her robe she slipped it on then hurried down to the beach. She would not swim. Swimming alone was too dangerous. But she patted oil onto her tan skin and stretched on the warm sand and let the feel of sun against her body lull her into a half sleep. She turned over once and let her backside toast for a while.

After an hour or so she rinsed the sand from her skin then climbed the wooden stairs back to the villa. The Mercedes was back in the driveway, but she saw nobody about. She hurried on to her room.

Megan closed her door and after she showered and toweled herself with a mint-colored bath sheet she stretched out on the cool satin-sheeted bed for a short nap. She was enjoying the sea breeze wafting through the window and over her body and beginning to doze when she heard low voices. Two women were speaking. Megan guessed they were sitting on the patio which was almost directly under her window.

"*Por Dios!* What a handsome man, Maria! Every time he looks at me with those dark eyes I feel faint all over. If he were just to ask me once—"

"Well, he's not going to ask you anything, Tia. Those dark eyes are for nobody but Miss Delgado."

"Oh, pooh! Jacques Ducruet is still playing the field. He just lets the sultry Yolanda think she is the one and only in his life. Rosa said he tried to kiss her last year in the pantry, but she put up a fight."

"Rosa dreams on." Maria laughed. "I saw Jacques and Yolanda just last week down at the beach. Yolanda didn't have to make up dream stories. And she doesn't wear those fancy swimsuits Jacques keeps in every bedroom. She doesn't wear . . . any."

"Maria! You'll get yourself fired if anyone hears you talking that way. What were you doing at the beach? Spying on them?"

Maria laughed. "I got me a boyfriend too, Tia. Not much place on an island to go except to the beach. I wasn't spying. But Yolanda Delgado isn't the only one Jacques brings to the cove. I've seen him there with others. And they're all beautiful. I don't know where he finds such women."

Tia snorted and slapped something down onto the table. "Such women find him. I hear there's another one after him right now."

"Who?"

"Don't know. But she's in the green room. Someone said Jacques had her out on his yacht last week. I'd hate to be in her shoes if Yolanda finds out."

"I wouldn't have minded being in her shoes on the yacht."

Megan sat up as she realized the women were talking about her. And how false their gossip was! If only they knew. Yet their words about Jacques and Yolanda stung her deeply. They had a ring of truth that she couldn't deny. Megan flung herself back onto the bed in despair. She was in love with Jacques. Could she bear to live her life without him? She must. She would never give him the satisfaction of throwing her over for Yolanda or for anyone else who caught his roving eye.

After a while Megan rose and dressed. She went to the kitchen and reported to Juanita her conversation with Yolanda.

"Is there no way that I can help with the preparations?" she asked. "I'm here to work. Yolanda is paying me well for my services."

"I've brought in the extra girls to help," Juanita said. "There is nothing you need do but oversee the arrangements. Give your okay to my work to Yolanda. That would help me the most."

That evening Megan ate with the bevy of servant girls and listened while Juanita issued their orders. She wished she knew which two were Maria and Tia. And was Rosa present? Had Jacques really tried to make love to her? There was no way of knowing which girl was which. They were all big-eyed and silent. Juanita did all the talking.

Megan made brief notes on the orders Juanita gave the extras. She would present the high points to Yolanda, should Yolanda ask for specific details. In the back of her mind she doubted that Yolanda would ask. Yet perhaps she would. Perhaps she would ask in order to impress Jacques with what a fine job she was doing for the charity drive.

After dinner Megan retired to her room, glad to be alone, yet feeling lonely. There was nothing for her to do here on Contadora. She felt like a person in exile. She was a bother to Yolanda in Panama so Yolanda had shipped her to a place where she would be out of the way. Yet she had a feeling that although she was out of Yolanda's sight she was not out of her mind.

As Megan stretched out on the pale green sheets and listened to the sound of the surf pounding the shore, she pretended Jacques was there beside her, lying by her side, turning his head to kiss her hair, her brow, her cheek, and finally her expectant, parted lips. The rhythmic hammering had a hypnotic effect, yet it failed to put her to sleep, nor did the heady scent of the rose in the crystal vase. She sat up and tried reading a bit from a magazine she had picked up in the hotel lobby before she had left Panama.

When at last her eyelids felt heavy, she snapped off the bedside lamp and tried to sleep. But sleep still refused to come. When her head began to ache she rose and dressed. After slipping into slacks and shirt she grabbed a pair of sandals and tiptoed from her room. Perhaps a walk along the private beach would tire her and make sleep possible.

The beach path near the villa was dark with shadows, but the steps leading down to the water were awash with moonlight. Megan felt the rough railing beneath her fingers as she watched the surf surge and curl against the shoreline. The night smell of the water reminded her of the living marine world she couldn't see.

Now she felt the grainy sand work into her sandals. It still carried the sun's warmth although many hours of darkness had passed. Megan walked to a cove where a ridge of rock rose high above her head. The moonglow made her feel spotlighted and exposed, so she circled the rocks until she reached the shadowed side. Dropping onto the sand, she leaned back against the still-warm rock and gazed toward the horizon.

Moonlight turned the world a silvery gray and Megan

stared at sky and sea until she felt thoroughly drowsy. "Surely I'll be able to sleep now," she murmured half aloud. Rising, she kept to the shadows as long as she could, then she walked across wet sand toward some seagrape trees in the distance.

A narrow path through the seagrape and palms led back to the villa. Here dry leaves crunched underfoot. Suddenly she sensed that she was no longer alone. She paused on the path and heard footsteps behind her. Who? Had someone followed her from the villa? José? Or perhaps it was Tia and her boyfriend.

Not wanting to interrupt any lovers Megan began walking faster. She had thought nighttime strolling would be safe in such a secluded spot on private property. The footsteps behind her speeded up. She slowed. The footsteps slowed. Remembering her frightening experience in Panama Megan felt a chill feather across the nape of her neck and her heart pounded.

Someone definitely was following her. At first she was tempted to call out, to let the intruder know she was aware of his presence. His? Why was she so sure the follower was a man? Maybe Juanita was sleepless too. Responsibility for Yolanda's gala would be enough to keep anyone awake.

But if a man was nearby, why let him know she was aware? Her best move would be to make a dash for the safety of the villa. Through the trees she could see the wooden steps leading to the house. Now they were half shadowed. If she ran she could reach them in a few seconds. It seemed to be her wisest choice of action.

Pausing a moment before taking flight, Megan tried to sight a sure course to her goal. Once she zig-zagged through the palms and seagrape she would face an area of smooth dry sand that lay between her and the steps.

There would be no protection there. Speed would be her only ally.

Grabbing a deep breath Megan left the path through the trees. She tripped over roots and rocks, sounding like a tank crashing through the underbrush.

"Stop!" a hoarse voice called out.

Megan kept on running. Did the voice belong to José? The one word gave her no clue. She forced herself to run faster. Her side ached and her lungs felt as if they might burst from the sudden exertion.

When she reached the dry sand Megan was surprised at how deeply her sandals sank into it. It sucked at her feet, holding her back, slowing her escape.

"Stop, I say!"

Megan felt a strong hand grip her arm and spin her around. Ducking her head she tried to jerk free. For a moment she almost succeeded. Her captor lost his grip on her arm and she dashed toward the villa, but she had taken only three steps when strong arms tackled her and she fell helpless onto the ground.

Sand gritted into her right cheek and she tasted dust and blood on her tongue. As she opened her mouth to scream a hand clamped over her lips, closing off all sound.

"Megan! What are you doing prowling the grounds at this hour?" Jacques's words hit her eardrums like stones, and instead of being able to relax, she grew more tense.

"Jacques! You frightened me." Her voice shrilled.

"Quiet!" Jacques clamped his hand over her mouth again. "You want to wake the servants? I saw you skulking about in the shadows and I thought you were an intruder."

Megan clawed Jacques's hand from her mouth. "And I'm supposed to believe you were patroling the beach for intruders! You knew I was at the villa. You knew I liked to walk. You followed me deliberately."

Jacques pushed her back onto the soft sand, pinning her arms above her head with one hand. He covered her body with his, pressing close until she felt his skin warm against hers. Her lips reached to meet his, and she felt herself relax with a sigh to respond to the fierce demand of his lovemaking. When he had kissed her breathless, he rolled to one side to kiss her eyelids, her cheeks, her throat. As she clung to him, she could feel his hand cup her breast then glide down to round her slender waist, her smooth hips. Involuntarily her trembling fingers explored his chest, his tapered waist, the long muscled thighs that gripped hers.

"And you say you don't care for me," Jacques whispered huskily in Megan's ear as his fingers traced the curve of her cheek. "If there is anything that I can't stand, it's a liar." His voice was mocking.

Megan forced herself to a sitting position. "Why should I bother to lie to you?" she demanded, angry that her all too willing body had betrayed her feelings.

"I suppose you think you've made a great conquest. You scare me half to death then you force yourself on me. You're a real gentleman, Jacques. You should be proud of yourself."

"You came out here to tempt me," Jacques accused. "You got exactly what you wanted."

"I didn't know you were on the place. I thought you were totally involved with Yolanda in Panama. You have taken unfair advantage of me."

"I have only returned to my home," Jacques pointed out. "I had no way of knowing you were prowling on my beach. Sometimes servants come skulking about hunting for something to steal that they can turn into quick cash. In those pants you looked like a boy . . .

from a distance. I think you deliberately set out to trap me."

"Poor innocent lad." Megan spat the words. "These pants and this shirt are hardly my man-trapping clothes. I know they're certainly not your kind of thing. You like your women a little less covered, don't you?"

"Care to try me and see?" Jacques pulled her to him and kissed her again. This time Megan forced herself to refrain from responding.

"Let yourself go, Megan. You know you want me as much as I want you."

"I don't want you or your kisses. I wish I could get that message through to you. And you don't want me either. You just want another conquest. Some men thrive on breaking hearts."

"I've broken your heart?"

"Of course you haven't. And you never will. My heart is very shatter-proof."

"But you love me. You were furious last night when you saw me swimming with Yolanda, weren't you?"

"How did you know I was . . ." Megan gasped.

"How did I know you were watching?" Jacques laughed. "I saw you, of course. Did you think you were invisible just because you were up on that high balcony?"

"I hate you, Jacques. I really and truly hate you."

"You love me. You're in love with me. Do you truly think that I have had so little experience with women that I cannot tell when a woman loves me? Why else would you ensconce yourself in my villa and throw yourself at my head whenever you got a chance? No, no, my dear, a girl like you does not make love with such abandon for a man she does not care for."

Megan's hand flew up and she would have slapped Jacques had he not caught her wrist and stopped the blow. "I . . . I hate you, Jacques. I really do. You're only interested in women and money. And not necessarily in that order. You're trying to use me to make Yolanda jealous. That's the only reason you came here tonight."

Jacques threw back his head and laughed at her. "What a joke! Make Yolanda jealous. I'm practically fighting Yolanda off with a stick as it is. If it weren't for the charity drive, the advertising, I'd . . . Don't you realize I came here tonight to bring Juanita the party supplies so she would have them early tomorrow morning? Yolanda!"

"Oh, sure. A lot you care about Juanita."

"Why are you so narrow-minded, Megan? Relax a little."

"If you think I'm going to throw off my clothes and make love to you in the sand like all your other women you're sadly mistaken." Megan stood, and Jacques made no move to stop her. Feeling rather foolish she began walking toward the steps.

Jacques followed her at an unhurried pace. "You're really impossible, Megan Taylor. You think everyone should believe as you believe. I think you're the one who worships money. You believe that one cannot give to charity without giving money."

"I can't think of anything that speaks louder than money." Megan flounced on toward the house.

"What about love?" Jacques called after her.

"How can you talk about love when all you really know about is lust?" Megan flung the words over her shoulder as she ran up the steps and into the villa. She dashed up the spiral stairs and into her room, closing and locking the door behind her.

She half expected to hear Jacques following her. But the villa was silent.

Chapter Fifteen

Megan thought she wouldn't sleep again that night and she was surprised when the sun shining through her window wakened her the next morning. She rose and dressed, then she packed her bag. Her return flight to Panama left at mid-afternoon and she planned to spend the morning with Juanita. Surely now that the supplies were here she would need help in getting preparations for the following evening's gala underway.

As Megan left her room she almost collided with Jacques in the hallway. He was dressed in white shirt and slacks and the dark smudges under his eyes only added to his appearance.

"You were waiting for me," Megan said. "How dare you!"

"You flatter yourself, Megan. It's breakfast time. I am merely headed toward the patio where I always have my coffee and eggs at this hour of the day. I'm glad to see that you're up and about. We'll be flying back to the hotel around ten o'clock."

"I have a reservation on the mid-afternoon commercial flight. Yolanda is expecting me then."

"Sorry, Megan. Plans have changed. I have orders from Yolanda that you are to return with me this morning. I don't think she trusts us here together at the villa."

Megan stepped in front of Jacques and started on down the spiral of steps. "I certainly can't blame her for that. She knows you well, doesn't she?"

147

"And you also, my dear. Even I didn't know you had a predilection for moonlit beaches until last night. You do remember last night, don't you?"

Megan felt her face flush and she was glad her back was to Jacques. She hurried on down the stairs and out onto the patio where Juanita was serving breakfast.

"*Buenos días,* Señorita, Señor." Juanita smiled directly at Megan, then gazed over Megan's shoulder at Jacques. "Do sit down and let me pour you some chilled orange juice. The bacon and eggs will be ready in a few minutes."

"There's no hurry, Juanita," Jacques said. "You know I always enjoy a leisurely breakfast. And I'm sure Miss Taylor does too."

"We cannot be too leisurely this morning, Señor," Juanita said, pouring the juice into chilled glasses misted white with frost. "Already José has gone to fetch the extra ladies who will help me in the kitchen today and tomorrow. Some have even spent the night here."

"Ah, yes." Jacques smiled. "The gala. For a moment it slipped my mind. Miss Taylor and I will be out of your way soon. My plane will be ready at ten o'clock."

"But I will help you until then, Juanita," Megan said, seating herself in the shade of the yellow umbrella. "Just show me what to do."

"Eat your fill first," Juanita said. "Then we will discuss the work."

Megan all but gulped her juice and coffee and she hardly tasted the eggs and toast. Jacques unnerved her this morning and she was ever conscious of his gaze as she pretended to devote her full attention to her meal. How much longer could she keep up her pretense that she didn't care for him? In three days her job with Yolanda would end. She had to last out those three days if she planned to keep her self-respect. If only she could forget the salt taste of his lips last night, his hands caressing her body.

"Have you ever seen such a beautiful sea?" Jacques asked, looking at Megan pleasantly over the rim of his coffee cup.

"It is beautiful," Megan agreed noncommittally.

"But not as beautiful by sunlight as by moonglow, right?"

Abruptly Megan picked up her empty dishes and headed for the kitchen. There was no way Jacques could force her to sit and chat with him. There were many things to be done, and she was eager for Juanita to put her to some work that would occupy her mind as well as her body.

"Through so soon?" Juanita met her in the doorway to the kitchen. "The breakfast was satisfactory?"

"It was delicious, Juanita. But now I'm ready to work. What can I do that will be of the most help to you? I'm really sorry that Yolanda has requested my presence back at the hotel this morning."

"With all my extra helpers I will manage nicely," Juanita said. "José has set up the buffet table against the east wall. Perhaps you would arrange the cloth and cut flowers for the centerpiece?"

"I'd love to." Megan walked to the long buffet table and unfolded the cloth that lay on one end of it. The cocoa-brown fabric blended with the paneling in the room, and as Megan unfolded it and spread it into place she tried to visualize the flowers she would need.

"I plan to use this silver bowl for the flowers," Juanita said. "A candelabra will stand on either side."

"What flowers do you prefer?" Megan asked.

"Yolanda has ordered that we use pale gold hibiscus from the bushes near the front entry. I have pale yellow candles for the candelabra."

"That sounds lovely, Juanita. But I can't arrange the

flowers today. The hibiscus blossoms are so fragile. They would be withered before tomorrow night. Shall we let the flowers go until tomorrow?"

"*Sí*, Señorita. A good plan. I was not thinking clearly."

By then José had returned with the extra helpers and Spanish chatter flowed from the kitchen. "Señorita Megan, would you be so good as to help with the casseroles? Just to oversee the cooking of the broccoli and the rice, yes?"

"Of course, Juanita." Megan smiled, glad that she knew her way around the kitchen as well as around an office. She helped a servant girl measure out the rice and water, add a pinch of salt, and set it on the stove to boil. Then she oversaw the cleaning of the broccoli. When it was ready she placed it on an aluminum rack to steam in a huge roaster.

"My, my but aren't we domestic?" Jacques's voice coming from behind her made Megan start in surprise. "There seems to be no limit to your talents, Megan."

"I'm merely making myself useful," Megan retorted. "Why don't you do the same? I understand that you love to cook."

"Only for two. Not for a crowd."

"I should have known." Megan turned the blaze under the broccoli a bit higher. Steam had begun to rise from the cooking pots and she felt perspiration beading on her forehead and her upper lip. When she turned to face Jacques, he was talking with one of the servants, but he winked at her as though they shared a conspiracy.

Megan kept her eye on the timer and when the rice was done she showed the servant girl how to drain it, rinse it, and set it aside to cool. Together they repeated the process ten times. Juanita planned ten casseroles for the guests.

It was almost ten o'clock before the rice and broccoli had been arranged in the casserole dishes and the cheese sauce added. Megan was almost glad when Jacques strode toward her with a glance at his wrist watch.

"Come, Megan. Let me take you away from all this."

Megan scowled and went to find Juanita who was showing another girl how to roll a cheese ball in chopped parsley and grated pecan meats.

"*Gracias*, Señorita Megan. You have been a great help to me. I will tell Miss Delgado when she asks."

"Thank you, Juanita. I wish I could stay longer, but I must leave."

Juanita walked with Megan and Jacques to the Mercedes and José drove them the short distance to the airstrip. He carried their bags across the blacktop to the plane, and Jacques helped Megan aboard then pulled himself up and into the pilot's seat. For a moment, he let his hand rest on her knee as if to keep his balance, but when Megan glanced at him, he grinned, and she knew his touch had been intentional. In spite of herself, it pleased her to know that Jacques enjoyed touching her.

She fastened her seatbelt and tried to pretend that she wasn't afraid as Jacques taxied down the runway. The plane rose, the force of the takeoff pinning her against the seat. The feeling reminded her of Jacques pinning her against the moonlit sand. Almost against her will she looked down at the trees, the beach, the sea.

"You're doing better," Jacques said. "You used to turn pea green. This time you kept it to a mild shade of mist gray."

Megan pulled a book from her shoulder purse and pretended to read. Jacques concentrated on the plane controls, and within a few minutes they were landing in

Panama. As attendants came to care for the plane, Jacques helped Megan to the ground. They walked toward the terminal and he linked his arm through hers, grinning down at her. She felt that she should pull away, but she couldn't. She could not resist the warmth of his arm against hers. And she recognized the clean odor of his skin—a male odor that was in no way masked by the lime scent he always wore.

"We do make a handsome couple, Megan. If you'd only smile and gaze into my face someone might start a rumor that we're a twosome."

"You're trying to make Yolanda jealous, aren't you?" Megan held her breath against the stale smoke stench as they passed through the terminal. "You don't care if your antics get me fired. You wouldn't care a bit. How can you be so self-centered!"

"I guess it comes naturally." Jacques grinned mischievously as he hailed a taxi for them. They sped toward the hotel.

As Megan flounced past the fountain and on across the hotel lobby to the elevator she suddenly thought of her grandmother. Gram always said that when two people were at odds with each other the one who walked two paces ahead was the one most angry. She consciously slowed down until Jacques was at her side.

They didn't speak on the short ride up to the Yolanda suite, but when Yolanda answered Jacques's knock she had plenty to say to both of them.

"And where have you two been?" Yolanda tapped her wrist watch with her forefinger. "You are late."

"We got caught in a traffic jam, Yolanda." Jacques grinned down at her, tilting her chin up with his forefinger. "The sky was full of pelicans all making left turns. I did my best, but sometimes one must wait one's turn with patience."

"Today is not a day for waiting." Yolanda did not smile at Jacques's attempt at humor. "There is too much to be done." Turning to Megan, she asked, "The gala? How's it going?"

"Juanita has everything under control. José has brought in extra help and all plans are progressing nicely. I should like to have stayed and been of more help."

"Let me decide where you'll be of help." Yolanda's gown swished as she crossed the room. "This morning, or what is left of it, we must plan our costumes for the gala."

"Oh, Yolanda! You didn't tell me the gala was to be a costume party."

"It's not a costume party. By costume I mean our gowns. We must plan carefully what we will wear. We must impress our patrons."

Megan felt a rush of blood to her face and neck. When she saw Jacques grinning at her, she looked away, refusing to watch him laugh at her misunderstanding.

"This morning we will go shopping to choose our gowns," Yolanda said. "I have made the appointment."

"But I've brought a long gown with me," Megan said, hoping to avoid the expense entailed in purchasing an evening gown of Yolanda's choosing.

"Perhaps you will model it for us now," Yolanda said. "I will decide if it is appropriate."

"I have important business elsewhere," Jacques said, backing toward the door. "I'll see you two lovely ladies later."

Yolanda darted to stand in front of the door. "No, Jacques. No. You must stay here. You must help us decide on our gala gowns. Your opinion I value most highly and I'm sure Megan shares my feeling, don't you, Megan?"

Megan felt Jacques's sardonic gaze although she refused to meet his eyes. "I trust your judgment, Yolanda. I'm sure you know what's best."

For a moment Yolanda smiled, but she still stood blocking the exit. "I appreciate your loyalty, Megan. But do slip on your gown for me . . . and for Jacques." She bridled. "I like a male reaction to help me form my opinion."

Feeling trapped, Megan retreated to her quarters, closing the door behind her. Her jade green gown was on the hanger where she had left it. Would Jacques tell that he already had seen it on her?

Quickly she peeled off her work clothes and slipped into the gown. She had chosen the pattern for its elegant simplicity, and now she smoothed the lace bodice with its boat-shaped neckline over her breasts. As she pulled up the back zipper she felt the satin skirt snug against her waistline, her hips. The gown was a perfect fit. Checking her appearance in the mirror she slipped into high-heeled barefoot sandals, before stepping back into the sitting room where Yolanda and Jacques were waiting.

"Ahhh!" Jacques breathed the sigh of approval. "You have chosen a clever secretary, Yolanda. Megan doesn't need the help of Dior or Mr. Dino. I would say her gown is perfect on her."

Megan looked at the air a bit to the left of Jacques's head, determined not to swallow his flattery that she felt was an ill-concealed attempt to stimulate Yolanda's jealousy.

Now Yolanda leaned against the door to the suite as if she was afraid Jacques might try to escape. She scrutinized Megan, her gaze traveling slowly from the

curve of her breasts down to the sandals that accentu-
ated the high arch and trim ankles.

"I really don't know, Megan." Yolanda cocked her
head to one side. "The fabric is nice, of course, but the
workmanship. . . . Perhaps it would be better to buy
you a new gown. I would not want the guests to whisper
behind my back that my secretary looks . . . frumpy."

Megan gritted her teeth. Was a job really worth this
humiliation? Frumpy! Indeed!

"Perhaps Yolanda is right, Megan," Jacques said.
"She has a practiced eye when it comes to judging other
women's clothing. Why not let her choose you a gown
from Dior's? She will pay. She won't notice the extra
expense, and you'll have the fun of wearing a high-
fashion gown that is one of a kind."

"This gown I have on is one of a kind."

"Come!" Yolanda said. "It's settled. We'll go to Dior
for our gowns."

"Not me," Jacques said. "I have a long-standing
appointment."

"But you must come," Yolanda said. "Break your
other appointment."

Jacques glanced at his watch. "I will go with you for a
few minutes if it is that important to you."

"It is important." Yolanda linked her arm through
Jacques's. "Come. We must go. My driver and my car
are waiting."

"I can't go this way." Megan glanced down at her
long gown.

"Then hurry and change," Yolanda said. "Meet us in
the lobby in five minutes."

Megan breathed a sigh as Yolanda and Jacques left
the suite. How could she cope! Clearly Jacques enjoyed
making Yolanda jealous. Was she more passionate
when she was stirred by jealousy? An unbidden picture

flashed into her mind. Two alabaster statues stood by the pool; they came closer together to blend in an embrace. . . . No, Yolanda would never allow Megan to choose her own gown. She would force her to wear something as unbecoming as she could find for her. But what did it matter if she were forced to wear a dress that she hated for one evening? She would only wear it once before leaving Jacques and Yolanda forever.

Megan slipped into her skirt and blouse. Reaching the hotel lobby she saw Yolanda and Jacques waiting out front in Yolanda's Continental. When she approached the limousine the driver alighted, opened the door for her, and helped her into the back seat beside Yolanda.

They drove through the heavy traffic in the banking district, passed El Panama Hotel, then turned onto Via España and drove until they reached the exclusive shops set far back from the street. Here the sidewalks were uncrowded, and the driver parked the limousine in a space marked 'reserved'.

"Won't you be towed away?" Megan asked, turning to Yolanda.

Yolanda chuckled. "Of course not. Other people might be towed off. But this special spot is reserved for the Yolanda Delgado party today. Come, let's go into the shop."

"Looks like you're out of luck, Yolanda," Jacques said, turning to face her. "The window shades are drawn. It is the siesta."

"It is the siesta hour for others, Jacques. For Yolanda Delgado it is a shopping hour. The store is open to us. Special models will show us a selection of gowns. We will have the store all to ourselves because I have arranged for it."

Megan was surprised, but what Yolanda said was

true. Yolanda knocked on the locked door of the shop. In a moment someone lifted the woven-reed shade, peeked out, then unlocked the door.

Chapter Sixteen

"Miss Delgado!" A tall Spaniard bowed from the waist then welcomed Yolanda and her party.

Megan welcomed the coolness of the silent store. The fragrance of Chanel No. 5 hung in the air. In the next moment the escalator mechanism began to hum and the steps began to move and somewhere in the distance the music of a string orchestra masked the escalator sounds.

"We are expecting you, Señorita," the Spaniard said. "Please follow me."

The man stepped onto the escalator and Yolanda followed him. Megan and Jacques joined them. At the top of the steps their host led them into a small room where three satin easy chairs were positioned in front of a carpeted stage. After they were seated the man took his place at the side of the platform, the music grew louder, and a model appeared wearing a reed-slim dress of scarlet silk and dangling a wisp of pink cape from the forefinger of her left hand.

The host's voice droned on pointing up the costume's fabric, design, price. Yolanda began taking notes, but Jacques just made himself more comfortable in his chair, enjoying the models and their posturings.

After a half-hour Megan began to wonder when the

modeling would stop. Now she understood why Yolanda had bothered to take notes. They had seen at least a dozen different costumes, each one more elegant than the preceeding one. Yet, when the modeling stopped and the host asked which gowns they wanted to try on, Megan had little trouble making a decision.

"I would like to try the peach-colored silk," Yolanda said.

"Of course," the host replied, bowing to Yolanda. He escorted her to the dressing room to the left of the platform, asking a fitting lady to assist her.

"Which gown did you prefer?" Jacques asked Megan as they waited.

"The leaf-green chiffon."

"The flowing skirt will set off your gracefulness." Jacques winked. "And I've always liked bodices gathered on an elastic. They have a charm all their own, don't you think?"

Megan looked away from Jacques, sorry she had confided her dress choice to him. He started to speak again, but just then Yolanda appeared on the platform, swung her hips just enough to set the shimmering silk in motion.

Megan gasped in spite of herself. "Oh, Yolanda, that gown is perfect on you!"

Yolanda smiled and slunk across the platform with the same hips-forward-shoulders-back gait that the models had used. "You mean that Yolanda is perfect for the gown, don't you?"

"Either way," Jacques said, "Either way, Yolanda. The gown is for you. It *is* you."

"I never choose the first gown I try on," Yolanda said. "Please wait and give me your opinion of others."

Jacques sighed, resignedly. Megan refrained from

sighing. She really didn't mind watching Yolanda model as much as she minded being in Jacques's presence for so long.

Yolanda next tried on an avocado green in a slinky jersey fabric with a dipping hemline. The bodice had a high neckline but a front slit opened when she moved to reveal much bustline.

"Bravo!" Jacques called as Yolanda swaggered across the platform. "That one is the real you, Yolanda."

"Doesn't she ever get angry when you tease her?" Megan snapped.

"She doesn't realize she's being teased, Megan. Yolanda takes such things as gowns and galas very seriously. That one would joke about either is beyond her understanding."

They watched while Yolanda modeled nine of the twelve gowns the models had shown them. At last she reappeared in her street dress and joined them with a helpless yet pleased expression.

"Which one, Jacques? I need your help. Which of the gowns did you like best? I will buy to suit your taste."

"I liked them all, Yolanda. You looked glamorous in each one of them. Perhaps you should buy them all."

Yolanda considered that suggestion for a moment as if she really might do just that. Then she shook her head. "Which gown did you like best on me, Megan?"

"The green jersey, I believe," Megan said honestly.

"Then I believe I'll buy the peach-colored silk." Yolanda grinned at Megan. "You don't think I'd let a rival choose my gown, do you? Really now."

"I didn't know you considered me a rival, Yolanda. A rival for what, pray tell?"

"All women are my rivals," Yolanda said. "Please do not take my comment personally."

For a moment Megan almost felt sorry for Yolanda. Surely it would be frightening to imagine every woman in the world as a rival.

"Now it's your turn, Megan," Jacques said. "Yolanda has chosen the peach silk. Which of the other creations do you want to try?"

Now the host was standing in front of Megan, offering his well-manicured hand to help her to her feet. Megan stood unassisted, but she glanced at Yolanda for instructions.

"Go ahead, Megan. Pick out the gown of your choice. I want our guests to know that Yolanda Delgado's secretary wears the best. One must keep up appearances at all times, you know."

"Perhaps you could arrange to have the label stitched to the outside of the gown," Jacques said. "That way nobody would be left in doubt as to the quality of your taste."

"No," Yolanda said. "I really think that would be unwise."

Jacques winked at Megan, but she pretended not to see the wink as she followed their host and joined a fitting lady in the satin-lined dressing room.

"I'm guessing that the Señorita wants to try the leaf-green chiffon," the lady said. "It would be perfect on you."

"You're right. Of all the gowns modeled, that one is my choice. I do hope it fits."

"If it doesn't fit, we can make it fit," the lady replied, touching the pins and scissors lying on a small table nearby. "But I don't think you have to worry. You have a perfect figure."

The lady eased the dress over Megan's head and patted it into place. "It feels right," Megan said.

"And it looks right. Go show your friends."

Megan walked onto the platform, conscious of Jacques devouring her with his gaze. "I like this gown, Yolanda. With your permission it will be my choice."

Yolanda cocked her head to one side and thrust out her lower lip in a gesture that Megan knew suggested disapproval. "I don't know, Megan. Perhaps you are a trifle too endowed in the hips for that gown. And perhaps not enough endowed in the bustline to do the fabric justice."

Megan felt her stomach knot in anger but she said nothing.

"Really, Yolanda," Jacques said. "The gown is perfect on Megan and you know it. Perhaps that's the trouble. *You know it.*"

Yolanda's eyes blazed as she ignored both Jacques and Megan and faced the fitting lady. "Show Miss Taylor the scarlet sheath, please. I think that dress would suit her."

Megan said nothing as she followed the lady back to the fitting room. She could see Yolanda's plan and she knew there was exactly nothing she could do about it. With her reddish hair she would look horrible in the scarlet gown.

"It will clash with your hair and your complexion," the lady said sadly. "Miss Delgado usually shows exquisite taste, but this time I don't understand her choice."

I do, Megan thought. She slipped into the sheath, modeled it on the platform, then stopped in front of Yolanda's chair.

"It's perfect on her," Jacques exclaimed.

Megan glared at Jacques and saw him wink at her yet again. What was he trying to do? Did he want her to be a laughing-stock at the gala!

"You're right, Jacques," Yolanda agreed. "The

scarlet is perfect on her. That's the gown we'll take. May we take them with us now?"

"Of course," their host replied. "I'll box them for you right away."

While the dresses were being wrapped Yolanda chose a silver chain studded with pearls and matching pearl earrings for herself. Then she chose a heavy gold chain for Megan. When they finished their shopping, Jacques carried their packages to the limousine and Yolanda's driver whisked them back to the hotel.

Megan spent the rest of the day writing letters to patrons, tallying up figures in the account books, and jotting down ideas Yolanda had for the gala the following evening. Jacques and Yolanda had dinner on the starlight roof while Megan called room-service to order her light supper on her balcony. She was thinking of retiring early when she heard Yolanda and Jacques enter the suite.

"How long will it take you to pack, Megan?" Yolanda called to her at the same time she rapped on her door.

"Pack for what?" At first Megan felt a chill of warning. Was Yolanda firing her? Had her work been unsatisfactory?

"I've decided we should fly to Contadora tonight. Jacques says the villa is in readiness, but I want to see for myself."

"But there are no flights until morning."

"Jacques will fly us over. Then we will be there to get a good grip on things in the morning. I'm sure Juanita will welcome our help. Can you pack right away and not keep us waiting?"

Megan sighed. She was not all that sure Juanita would be overjoyed to see them, but she said nothing. "You wish to leave within the hour?"

"Yes. Do pack quickly. Just pack something to wear around the villa tomorrow. Jacques will take our gowns on to his plane and get it ready for takeoff. My driver will drive us to the airport."

Megan set her supper tray aside and began packing as soon as Jacques left them alone. She hated the thought of a night flight across the sea, but what did it really matter? She would have to make the flight sooner or later. It might as well be sooner.

Megan was packed within twenty minutes, but she had to wait another twenty for Yolanda to get all her things together. Megan welcomed the ride through the balmy night to the airport. She was tired of being cooped up in the suite every night.

From the high hill where the hotel sat she looked out over the city at the lights glowing like millions of fallen stars. The sky was like a black bowl inverted to cover them. As always the air was fragrant with jasmine and the soft, humid touch of the sea breeze.

As the driver sped toward the airport Megan looked back at the hotel, its glowing lights rising into the sky until it looked like a beacon pointing out Panama to any weary traveler who might be searching for it.

The terminal at the airport was dark, but Jacques had arranged for the runway lights to be flashed on. He radioed to the control tower at Panama International some twenty miles away and received a go-ahead for takeoff.

The asphalt of the runway felt soft under Megan's feet and the faint odor of tar reached her nose as she walked toward the plane. Then the stench of diesel exhaust drowned out all other smells and Jacques helped her and Yolanda into the plane.

Their takeoff was smooth. For a while Megan peered down at the city lights below them, then all was blackness. She knew they were over the sea. Here and there she saw lights on small boats, but those were few and far between. Were there sharks in those waters? Of course there were. She shuddered. Would she never get used to flying! How could Yolanda seem so relaxed and at ease?

At last Megan felt the plane bank for a landing. She peered into the blackness below. No lights. How would Jacques find the landing strip? Her ears popped and she sensed that they were dropping lower and lower. At last she made out a dim light some distance from them. Then the plane touched down, bounced twice, and slowed. In moments Jacques taxied to a stop and when he opened the plane door José was running toward them ready to light their way to the Mercedes with a flashlight and a lantern.

"Buenas noches, Señor y Señoritas."

"Good to see you, José," Jacques said. "And thank you for guiding me in. The moonlight was almost enought light, but your lantern gave me clear direction."

Megan shuddered as she realized that Jacques had landed using nothing more for light than José's feeble lantern.

"You are an excellent pilot, Jacques," Yolanda said. "I always feel safe with you at the controls."

"Your confidence in my ability is heartwarming," Jacques said. "And you, Megan? You share Yolanda's feelings, of course."

"I'm afraid not. But I do appreciate your getting us here safely."

José led them to the Mercedes and Jacques rode up front with José leaving Megan and Yolanda in the back seat. Except for the lights at the guest hotel Contadora seemed totally blanketed in moonlight. Megan loved the remoteness of the island. Here one could really see the moon and enjoy the starshine. When they reached the villa José spoke.

"Everyone has retired for the night, Señor. If you need anything I will get it for you."

"Don't worry, José. *Gracias*. We will retire and rest up for a big day tomorrow."

"*Sí, Señor, gracias*," José said, bowing to them as he left.

Megan smelled jasmine at the doorway of the villa and after she had climbed the spiral stairs to her room and opened the window she could smell the sea and hear the breakers pounding on the shore. For a moment she stood at the window without turning on the light to watch moonlight silvering the sea and the sand. The breakers drowned out all other sound. She felt as though she were the only person in the world, a world that had been especially prepared for her this night.

At last she turned and snapped on a bedside lamp. To her surprise the simple but elegant room she had slept in the night before had been totally transformed. Megan stared in surprise at the books, the turntable, the records. And a TV. Yolanda knocked and entered before Megan could invite her in. "It's very nice in here," Yolanda said. "Very."

"I . . . yes." Megan refused to let Yolanda know that someone had fixed the room up for her. Jacques? Juanita? But maybe Yolanda did know. She was a frequent visitor here.

"I like for my help to work in comfort," Yolanda said.

"Then you arranged for the books, the TV?"

"No, I certainly did not arrange for it. Perhaps this room was intended for me. My room is quite plain."

"I'll be glad to change with you if it is important to you." How could Jacques have done this to her! Clearly he was still trying to make Yolanda jealous with no thought for Megan's job or her status with Yolanda. "Shall we make the switch tonight, Yolanda?"

"No. We will make no switch at all. The room is yours. Enjoy it."

Megan winced. Yolanda's haughty voice belied her words. She clearly was upset at the room arrangement and Megan guessed that she would pay for the oversight in the long run. Yolanda was not used to being second in anything.

Suddenly Megan's head began to ache and she wished Yolanda would leave her alone. "May I help you with something tonight, Yolanda? It's really quite late and we have much ahead of us tomorrow."

"There is nothing to do tonight," Yolanda said. "I've just come to wait here until Jacques delivers your gown. Then I will know you are properly settled."

And you'll know that Jacques has left me quite alone, won't you, Megan thought. If only Jacques would arrive, deliver the gown, and leave. Yolanda paced until a knock sounded on the door. When she opened it a look of surprise crossed her face. It was José and not Jacques who delivered the gown.

"Gracias, José," Yolanda said. "Muchas gracias."

José nodded and left them alone. Yolanda waited until Megan had hung the scarlet gown in her closet then she left. "Lock your door, Megan," she called over her shoulder. "With the villa full of servants, one never knows . . ."

"I'll take care, Yolanda."

After Yolanda departed Megan tried to settle down for the night. The sight of the scarlet dress that she would be forced to wear made her headache worse. She took two aspirin and tried to sleep, but again sleep evaded her. Rising, she slipped into her robe and headed downstairs to the patio. She would not walk, but surely there was no harm in sitting on the patio. And surely, if anyone else was up and about, she would not be taken for an intruder if she were merely sitting and minding her own business.

Megan sat in the full moonlight, staring out across the sea. Her head pounded with every slap of the surf. What if she was getting sick? The flu? What if she couldn't appear at the gala? Perhaps she was deliberately making herself sick with pent-up anger at Yolanda and at Jacques.

"It seems you're quite the night owl." Jacques's voice startled Megan, but she tried to hide her surprise.

"I thought nobody else was about. I have a headache and I thought fresh air might help it."

"Your scarlet gown has given you a headache?" Jacques laughed half to himself.

"The gown and . . . other things."

"What other things? Tell me. Perhaps I can help."

"My room, for instance," Megan stood and walked to the retaining wall.

"What about the room? If it is uncomfortable I'll see what can be done to improve it."

"Oh it's quite improved enough as it is. Books. Magazines. Radio. Record player. TV. And you intended for Yolanda to know, didn't you? You're using me, trying to make her jealous. Do you think I don't know what you're up to?"

Jacques laughed as he joined Megan at the retaining wall and stood looking out over the moonlit sea. "You flatter yourself again, Megan, if you think I have you so much on my mind. True . . . many things have been added to your room today. But not for your comfort. Not to make Yolanda jealous. In case it has slipped your mind I'd like to remind you that we're having a party here tomorrow. There will be dancing and crowds of people. Things have to be moved to make room for the festivities. The things in your room were placed there to make more room for the gala. Megan, sometimes your mind conjures up such wild thoughts that I have to laugh."

Suddenly all the wrongs of the day seemed to come to a climax inside Megan's head. Facing Jacques she shouted, "I hate you, Jacques. I really and truly hate you and your supercolossal conceit." She turned to flounce off, but Jacques grabbed her wrist and pulled her to him.

"Has anyone ever told you that you're beautiful when you're angry?"

"No." Megan spat the word. "Because I've never been this angry before. And your line is threadbare. It's on every late movie at least once an evening."

"But it just doesn't happen to be a line, Megan." Jacques pulled her to him in an embrace she couldn't escape. One arm encircled her waist while his other arm curled around her shoulder, gripping her flesh. When she felt his lips come down on hers she resisted only for a moment, then she yielded, feeling her arching body mold itself to his taut masculinity. *What difference does it make now,* she thought, *I am where I want to be at this moment. Tomorrow I will be out of this man's life and will never see him again.* She pressed her cheek against his chest and listened to his strong heart throb. Her senses swam as she inhaled the pleasant fragrance of his hair, his skin.

"Tell me you love me," Jacques said, looking down into Megan's eyes. "I want to hear you say the words."

Megan opened her mouth to protest just as Yolanda rushed across the patio, the heels of her mules slapping against the flagstones.

"So this is what goes on when my back is turned! So

this is how sweet Megan Taylor behaves when she thinks I am not looking. Miss Taylor, please return to your room at once."

Chapter Seventeen

Jacques stepped away from Megan, as surprised as she was at Yolanda's appearance and her angry outburst. Megan chose the moment to escape, following Yolanda's order to go to her room. How could she have allowed this to happen! It was all Jacques's fault for forcing his attentions upon her. No. Megan paused on the spiral of stairs. It was her own fault for responding so willingly to his lovemaking. How could she have been such a fool!

Megan had hardly reached the privacy of her room and flung herself across the soothing satin sheets on the bed when she heard Yolanda's angry tapping on the door. For a moment Megan was tempted to ignore the knocks, but she had to face Yolanda sooner or later. Postponing the scene would not help. Megan rose from the bed.

Yolanda burst into the room before Megan could open the door. A tendril of raven hair had escaped its silver comb and dangled limply on her neck. Her eyes blazed fire and her bosom heaved as she panted from the exertion of running up the stairs. Her gardenia scent invaded the room.

"Of course you are fired, you little . . ." Yolanda paused, searching for a word. "You'll leave this villa immediately. *Immediately*. You'll receive no pay. Your contract stated you would be paid only upon fulfilling your duties. You have failed at that. Pack! Now! Out of my sight!"

Megan stepped back, shaken by the force of Yolanda's anger.

"Easy, Yolanda." Now Jacques, still wearing a surprised expression, entered the room, stepping between Yolanda and Megan. "You have no right to order anyone from my villa. Megan may remain here as my guest if she so desires."

"And if she doesn't so desire?" Megan glared at Jacques, trying to ignore the way the overhead light gleamed on the tan of his arms.

"Then I'll drive you to the hotel for the night," Jacques said.

"I will drive her to the hotel," Yolanda said haughtily. "Megan is my problem. And she will be packed and out of the Yolanda suite of Hotel Ducruet before the noon tomorrow. Get your things, Megan. You are leaving this villa immediately."

"Leave me alone, Yolanda. I will remain here for the night as Jacques suggests and leave early in the morning. There is no need to cause a scene at the hotel tonight. Now will both of you please go?"

To Megan's relief Jacques took Yolanda's elbow and ushered her from the room. Megan closed the door behind them and this time she pushed the lock button securely in place. Peeling off her robe she strode to the shower and let cold water sluice over her body until her hot anger cooled and her teeth chattered. Then after toweling herself dry she stretched out on the bed and stared at the ceiling. Moments later she ignored the tapping on her door.

"Megan," Jacques called. "Megan, open up. I need to talk to you."

Megan covered her head with the pillow.

The next morning Megan began packing, leaving the crimson gown hanging in Jacques's closet. As she was tucking in her toothbrush and lip gloss a servant girl tapped on her door.

"I bring your breakfast, Señorita. Open please?"

Megan opened the door half expecting to see Jacques in the corridor, but the girl was alone. "Gracias, Señorita." Megan took the tray and closed the door once more.

Although she wasn't hungry Megan had finished the goblet of chilled orange juice and a small compote of diced papaya and lime juice before Yolanda knocked.

"Open, Megan. At once."

Megan took her time crossing the room, but she knew she couldn't stall. She opened the door and faced Yolanda. Although she wore a flamboyant crimson caftan, dark circles shadowed Yolanda's eyes and the skin of her face looked dry and fragile as tissue paper. Fine lines drooped from the corners of her mouth and her nostrils flared as she spoke.

"Jacques is at the airstrip waiting for us. Come along."

"Waiting for *us*, Yolanda?"

"You do not think I would allow you to fly with Jacques to Panama alone, do you? You do not think I would allow you to enter the Yolanda suite without my being present? Now that I know you are not to be trusted . . ."

"Let's go, Yolanda." Megan cut Yolanda's tirade short. Now that Yolanda no longer was her employer she felt no need to succumb to her verbal abuse, yet her own dignity of character kept her from speaking her mind and saying things she might regret later.

José drove them to the airstrip in the Mercedes, and they rode through the soft tropical morning in angry silence. Jacques helped them both aboard the Cessna then crawled into his own seat. As usual he wore white slacks and sport shirt that set off his tanned skin, but today Megan ignored him. She looked out the window at blue sky and a trail of windswept clouds, and nobody spoke during the flight to Panama nor during the taxi ride to Hotel Ducruet.

"I can't believe you're actually going to carry out your threat to fire Megan, Yolanda," Jacques said as they rode to the penthouse suite in the elevator. "It is quite unlike you to be so uncharitable. Please reconsider. Last night's incident was all my fault. I intruded on Megan's privacy. She had nothing to do with instigating what . . . happened."

"I saw very clearly exactly what Miss Megan had to do with that scene. She is through. Finished. I do not intend to change my mind."

Jacques opened the door to the suite and started to pace in front of a velvet couch. An odor of stale coffee hung in the room and Yolanda flung open a sliding door in the room that had been Megan's, then returned to stand beside one of her pictures.

"Out, Jacques!" Yolanda pointed to the door. "I will not have you interfering with me. Out!"

Megan saw a plum-colored flush rise beneath Jacques's tan, but he rose and stormed from the room. She smiled to herself at the thought of the powerful Jacques Ducruet being ordered from his own hotel suite.

"Pack quickly, Megan," Yolanda ordered. "I must return to the villa." Yolanda paced and as she paced she lighted a long brown cigarette in an ebony holder. Smoke wisped toward the ceiling, but Yolanda did not puff on the cigarette. She merely let it burn itself out.

"I have everything now," Megan said, snapping her suitcase shut.

Yolanda snorted and looked at her through narrowed

lids. "Everything? You are most mistaken. You still do not have Jacques. Think about that tonight wherever you are, Megan. Think of Yolanda dining and dancing with Jacques. As the saying goes—eat your heart out."

Megan strode toward Yolanda, but before she could open the door Yolanda pressed two quarters into her hand. "Bus fare, Megan. I simply can't bear the thought of you walking back to wherever it was you came from."

Bus fare indeed! Quietly Megan laid the coins on a coffee table, left the suite, and took the elevator to the hotel lobby. At the moment no taxis were present, so she walked down the hill toward the flowing avenue traffic and a bus stop a few blocks away. Had Yolanda deliberately shooed all the cabbies from sight?

Megan's right arm felt as if it had been stretched six inches longer than her left arm as she set her heavy suitcase down and waited for the next bus. She barely had time to flex her fingers to restore the blood circulation before Jacques pulled up at the curbing in his Mercedes.

"Taxi, ma'am?" he called through the open window.

Megan pretended not to hear.

"Don't be stubborn, Megan. Get in." Jacques leaned across the empty passenger seat and opened the car door. Megan looked in the other direction.

In one fluid movement Jacques slid across the car seat, alighted, then swooped Megan's suitcase onto the car's rear seat. Straightening, he seized her elbow and steered her toward the car. "Get in. No arguments. Just get in. I owe you an apology and I'm determined that you're going to hear me out."

Megan obeyed as if she had no will of her own. Maybe she had been wrong about Jacques. She had expected him to disappear from her life immediately, to announce his engagement to Yolanda at the gala, and to . . . to what? To live happily ever after. Surely it was time she quit believing in fairy tales, even those that concerned story-book people like Jacques and Yolanda. She wished the Mercedes didn't always smell of gardenia. She had always disliked their overpowering odor.

Jacques eased the car through traffic, heading for the old city. "You have my sincerest apology, Megan. Your predicament is entirely my fault. True, I was purposely goading Yolanda, but I never intended for you to be fired. You must believe that."

"Just what did you intend?"

Jacques paused. "I'm not quite sure. For a while I was trying to keep distance between myself and Yolanda. But last night I really intended to persuade you to tell me you loved me."

"I'm sorry your intentions went astray and I'm sure you and Yolanda can patch up your differences."

"Okay, Megan, I deserve your anger, but give me a chance to make amends. I have this whole day free. You would give me pleasure if you would allow me to spend it with you."

Now they were nearing the ruins of Old Panama and Jacques parked the Mercedes to the side of the area reserved for tour buses. Today no buses were present and the ruins were deserted except for two children playing tag and a calico cat stalking a fieldmouse across the mowed grass.

"Will you spend this day with me, Megan?"

"I should spend my day with a man who intends to announce his engagement to Yolanda?"

"That will not happen."

"Yolanda has called the engagement off? I'll never believe that."

Jacques didn't answer. Instead he left the car, walked around to Megan's side and opened the door. "Come, let's not spoil a lovely day talking about Yolanda."

Jacques's eyes were dark magnets drawing Megan from the car to his side. They strolled through the ruins of ancient Panama. Megan inhaled the scent of hay and spotted a large stable behind the ruins. A horse whinnied then all was silent again. Without speaking they climbed crumbling steps into the stone shell of a burned-out cathedral and sat together in a high archway that overlooked the crumbled foundations of the ancient buildings. Gray and brown stones, some blackened by fire and weathered by the elements, lay where they had lain for centuries. Megan couldn't help comparing Jacques to the ruthless Henry Morgan. She could almost smell the smoke from pirates' cannons still clinging to the sun-warmed boulders they sat upon.

"They saved the golden altar, you know," Jacques said at last. "When the citizens realized that Morgan was here to loot Old Panama, the faithful painted the golden altar in this cathedral with black paint. The pirates never guessed at the riches they overlooked. The altar's refurbished and set into a church in the new city."

"I know. Everyone knows that story. All the tour buses stop to let the tourists see the restored altar."

"I think it's a miracle that anyone could hide something so grand by merely painting it black." Jacques looked down at Megan and smiled. "But you have done the same thing, so perhaps it isn't such a miracle after all."

"What have I painted black?"

"Me. But of course if you'll take time to look, you'll find pure gold underneath."

Megan smiled in spite of herself, and Jacques took advantage of her moment of relenting. Pulling her toward him with one arm, he tilted her chin with his forefinger and kissed her with a soft gentleness she didn't dream was possible. His warm lips barely touched hers and his breath felt light and misty on her cheek.

Megan waited for the kiss to grow more demanding, but it did not. No one had ever kissed her with such sweetness and she felt her pulse pounding in her throat. She let her own lips part and as she did so Jacques drew away from her.

"I have a favor to ask, Megan."

"What is it?" Megan was half afraid of the answer, but to her surprise Jacques's reply was not even close to what she had expected.

"I want you to come with me to one of the Ducruet Enterprises."

"But why?" Megan blushed. "I thought perhaps you had something more romantic than business in mind. But with you it's always business, isn't it?"

"Not always, Megan. Not always. But will you come with me?"

"Where is this enterprise and what is it?"

"It's close by and it's a brickyard."

"A brickyard! How fascinating. Just the sort of place I've always wanted to visit on the day I've been fired from my first and only job."

"Good! Since it's what you've always wanted to do, I won't disappoint you. Let's go at once." Jacques put his hands around her waist and lifted her from the stone archway, then taking her hand he led the way down the crumbled steps to the ground.

"What are you thinking, Megan?" Jacques asked as he helped her into the Mercedes.

"It doesn't really matter to you, does it?" She wasn't about to tell him that she had decided to enjoy her last minutes with him no matter what. After today she knew she would never see him again so why not live it up? Why not enjoy the moment? She felt proud of herself for not revealing her love to him. But then why should she have? Jacques had never mentioned love to her. Perhaps he only knew passion. After today Jacques Ducruet would not matter to her in any way.

Jacques drove expertly through the traffic to an industrial area, then he threaded the Mercedes through the narrow streets to a clearing where modern sheds and huge, high-roofed buildings shimmered in the sunlight. Behind the buildings mounds of gray clay rose like mountains. The sign above the gate read: DUCRUET BRICK AND TILE. Megan smelled dust in the air and felt a slight grit on her tongue.

"Simply fascinating," she said, but she smiled as she spoke.

"Sarcasm will get you nowhere." Jacques helped her from the car and they walked to the office inside the brick fence that surrounded the work area. A slim Panamanian dressed in denim jeans and a blue chambray shirt sat behind the small desk that held a manual typewriter, a file basket, and a stack of sample brick. He rose as Jacques entered.

"*Buenos días,* Señor Ducruet."

"*Buenos días,* Pedro. I'd like for you to meet Miss Taylor." Megan and Pedro nodded greetings at one another. "Miss Taylor is interested in the brick business, Pedro. Tell her how many men we employ here."

Pedro tapped a pencil on the desk as he thought for a moment. "Twenty-five men, Señorita. That is about it."

"Twenty-five family men, right, Pedro?"

"Is right, of course. Family men."

"And you have a family yourself, do you not?"

"*Sí,* Señor. Manuelita and I have two sons and two daughters."

"And each child as handsome as you," Jacques said. "Thank you, Pedro. We'll walk around the grounds a bit if you don't mind."

"Of course, Señor."

Jacques led Megan over the brickyard where she saw more huge mounds of clay and an enormous kiln where the green bricks were baked. At the other end of the yard men using tongs placed bricks in wheelbarrows and wheeled them to a narrow-gauge railway.

"Twenty-five men, Megan. Think about that. Twenty-five men with families."

"What are you getting at, Jacques? I really don't understand. This is all very interesting, but . . ."

"This enterprise is possible only because I pour the profits from some of my other businesses into it. Ducruet Brick. This is my idea of a true and dignified charity—helping people help themselves. Think about that, Megan."

Megan watched a man operating a forklift loading brick onto a truck bed. "I don't understand how you can consider a profitable business a charity venture. Your reasoning eludes me."

"If Ducruet Enterprises didn't provide work for these men, where do you think they would be?" Jacques asked.

"Working somewhere else, I should think."

"Or working nowhere at all." Jacques snorted. "Panama's slums are full of able-bodied men who can't find work. All those men need is a chance in life. Panama is ripe for the growth of the brick industry, but someone has to provide the financial backing to get it going. That someone is me. I tell you providing jobs for people is my idea of a worthwhile charity. Not only do I provide a living for twenty-five men, but I also provide the means of supporting their families."

"I am not convinced that is charity." Megan laughed. "You are oh so kind, Jacques. Of course you expect no profit from this enterprise that will benefit yourself."

"Of course I expect a profit. That's what business is all about. Profit."

Megan wiped a smudge of dust from her skirt and wondered how Jacques managed to keep his outfit so spotless. "At least you're honest about the profit angle. But the way I see it profit is your big thing and you're using these men to gain your own ends."

Jacques scowled and for the second time Megan saw the plum-colored flush under his tan. "I've never known anyone so narrow-minded in all my life," Jacques said. Grabbing Megan's wrist he pulled her back to the Mercedes. "You are quite impossible, Megan Taylor."

Chapter Eighteen

"Get in the car," Jacques ordered. A thin white line between his upper lip and his nose warned Megan that she had roused hot anger in this man. Had she not known it was the last day she would ever spend with him she might have been afraid.

"Where are you taking me now?"

"To the airport."

"I want to go home."

"That can wait. We're returning to the villa. Yolanda hired you to help with tonight's gala and I intend to see that you render that service."

"But Yolanda fired me."

"And you don't have enough gumption to stick up for your own rights? You may be stubborn in your beliefs, Megan, but I feel sorry for you. I can't let Yolanda steam-roller you as she is doing."

"I don't need anyone to feel sorry for me."

"If you perform the work you contracted to perform Yolanda will have to pay you. If she refuses then you can consult legal counsel. Your firing was my fault, and I intend to see that you are reinstated."

"Oh, Jacques, for heaven's sake! Yolanda fired me and for good reason. I'll never resort to forcing myself on her. And why do you want me back at the villa? I'm the most narrow-minded person you've ever met. Remember those words?"

"How could I forget?"

"So take me home."

"No."

"Why?"

"May I tell you about my brother?"

"Why now?"

"His name is Michael. He's in a sanitorium."

"That's almost as fascinating as the brickyard."

"It's no joking matter."

"I'm sorry, Jacques," Megan said, feeling contrite. "I meant no ill will toward your brother. I'm snappish. It's just that everything seems wrong today. Tell me about Michael if you want."

"About twelve years ago when Michael and I were twenty-one or so, our parents gave each of us one million dollars to do with as we saw fit. I invested my million in various business enterprises here in Panama. I made some mistakes. I lost some of the million. But I also invested wisely in many cases. My capital grew."

"And Michael? What did he do with his million?"

"Michael turned playboy and gambler. The money meant little to him. He soon lost it to the gaming tables, to women. Then he began drinking to drown out his troubles. That money ruined him, Megan. It was charity even though it came from our parents. Michael didn't earn the money and in time it ruined him. That's why I don't believe in handing people money or free scholarships, no strings attached. Look what accepting such a gift did to Michael.''

Jacques looked so serious Megan almost laughed. "There's a great big flaw in your reasoning, Jacques. So maybe the million dollars ruined Michael. But what about you? You received a million dollars too. The freebie didn't ruin you. Quite to the contrary I'd say. And I accepted charity from my grandmother and it didn't ruin me. I planned to repay her from my earnings on this job. I've failed in that, but I will repay her. And soon. Giving people an education is just another way of giving them a way to help themselves, isn't it?''

Jacques thought for many moments then he laughed. "Touché. Perhaps you are right. Perhaps we both have been more than a bit narrow-minded in our concepts of charity.''

Now that Jacques had backed down on his rigid views Megan reconsidered her own thinking. "And perhaps you are right too, Jacques. Providing worthwhile employment for people is a fine thing to do. There really can be no growth without profit, can there? I think I'm beginning to understand.''

"Then you'll forgive me?''

"Forgive you for what?''

"For milking the Yolanda Drive for every bit of advertising for the Ducruet Enterprises that I could squeeze out?''

"You're forgiven.'' Megan leaned toward Jacques and kissed him lightly on the ear as he drove toward the airport.

"Now that all is well between us, let's be off to Contadora.''

"No. I want to go home.''

"And I want you at the party."

"Why?"

"This is my party as much as it's Yolanda's. And I want you in attendance."

"You're still trying to make Yolanda jealous and at my expense."

They rode in silence for many blocks and when they reached the airport Jacques pulled her toward him. "If reasoning won't make you see things my way, maybe this will." Now he kissed her with no tenderness at all. He pinned her head to the headrest as he brought his lips down on hers with a strength that sent chills coursing through her. She responded with a strength of her own, running her fingers through his hair, caressing his neck, his back.

"I knew you'd see things my way," Jacques said smugly, releasing her.

Megan gasped for breath and felt her whole body ache in a way she had never ached before, yet she would not give in to Jacques.

"I see things no differently than I did three minutes ago."

"But you're going to the villa with me, aren't you?"

"Yolanda will be furious."

"That's partly why you're going, isn't it?" Jacques chuckled and pulled the keys from the ignition. "You know Yolanda treated you unfairly. To return to the party with me as your escort will help salve your wounded ego, won't it?"

"You make me seem very base and vulgar."

"I enjoy base and vulgar women." Jacques grinned down at her, then hurried her to the plane. They had to wait a few minutes for permission to take off, and while they waited Jacques ordered them a light lunch to eat in the plane. As Megan ate she stared at her hand in her lap. What was all this leading to? Why was she going back to Contadora with a man who didn't love her to a party where she was not wanted?

She had let Jacques think she was going back to spite Yolanda, but she knew better. She was going because she was hopelessly in love with Jacques Ducruet, because she couldn't bear to give up the opportunity of being with him for these final few moments.

Their flight to Contadora was smooth, their landing was smooth, and even their ride with José back to the villa was smooth. Everything was smooth until they encountered Yolanda just inside the villa entry. She was still wearing the scarlet caftan and the cloying scent of gardenia surrounded her. Her eyes were like two dark wasps when she saw Megan.

"What are you doing back here?" Yolanda demanded. "You I have fired this very morning. Out! Out!"

Megan felt like retreating, but Jacques held her hand as he stepped between her and Yolanda.

"Hold it, Yolanda. Miss Taylor has not returned as your employee. She has returned as my guest for this evening's gala. Much of her effort has gone into the preparations for this party and I think she deserves to be in attendance. I want her here. Now if you'll stand aside, I'll show her to her room."

For once Yolanda was open-mouthed, and Megan thought that seeing Yolanda in that condition was worth whatever else might be in store for her this day. As far as she could see the gala boded nothing good. It would be her farewell to Jacques. She had loved and lost again, but at least this time the man she loved was unaware of her feelings. She still had her dignity.

The first thing Megan saw in her room was the green chiffon gown she had tried on in Panama lying across the green satin of the bed. A pair of matching sandals lay beside it in a nest of crumpled tissue paper, a string of pearls and a pair of pearl earrings lay on the pillow.

"What does this mean?" Megan asked. "How did these things get here?"

"I ordered them sent here, Megan. For you. What did you think I was doing all the time you were walking to the bus stop? I want you to wear that gown and those sandals tonight."

"But I can't afford such a gown, such slippers and jewelry. I've been fired, you know. And even if I could afford such finery it is not the way I would choose to spend my money."

"Perhaps you cannot afford the clothes, but I can. And I have purchased them. You will wear them because they were intended for you. Christian Dior must have had you in mind when he dreamed up that creation."

Megan stood at the foot of the bed. "I will not accept such an elaborate gift from a man . . . from a stranger."

The thin white line appeared again on Jacques's upper lip, and before Megan could sidestep him, he pulled her to him. With one arm around her waist and the other supporting her back he kissed her. For a moment he bit gently at her upper lip then he parted her lips with his tongue.

Megan felt the softness of the bed beneath her as she slid down onto it, Jacques's body pressing down on her. He kissed her again tenderly as he had kissed her in the arched window of the old cathedral. He kissed her eyes, her throat, the curve of her breast. When he finally withdrew his lips from her yielding flesh, she lay quietly for a moment, allowing the sweetness of his touch fade before profaning it with speech. When she spoke, her voice was whispery and weak.

"Let me go, Jacques. Please, let me go." Her tone belied her request.

"What's the hurry?" Jacques pinned her to the bed with one hand on her shoulder. "I want you to realize that I am a man, but that I am not a stranger."

"No." Megan smiled weakly, feeling her hair fanned back from her face. "You really aren't a stranger, are you?"

Jacques kissed Megan again, covering her lips with his until she felt a pleasant weakness flow through her body.

"I love you, Megan. I've never said those words to any woman before. I love you."

"And I love you, Jacques." The words had slipped out quite unbidden and almost immediately Megan wished she could recall them. She felt the blood rush to her neck, her face. Even the roots of her hair felt hot. She had done the thing she had vowed never to do. She had revealed her love to a man who did not care for her.

With a strong thrust she twisted free from Jacques's embrace and stood with her back pressed against the door. "Forget what I just said, Jacques. I didn't mean it. Whatever you sense that I feel for you is strictly physical. I am not emotionally involved at all. I'm sorry if I've misled you."

"But I love you, Megan. You don't hear me changing my mind."

"You merely feel sorry for me," Megan replied. "You feel sorry for me because I've been fired from a position important to me, because I have no lover, because I wear a false engagement ring to fool myself. I'll not have you feeling sorry for me."

Laugh lines appeared at the sides of Jacques's eyes. "So that ring *is* a phony. You'll never know how many times I hoped so. And you'll never guess how many times I've tried to find out who gave it to you. But that's all past now. I love you, Megan. Believe me."

"How do you expect me to believe you when I've seen you in action with Yolanda, when I read your name in the gossip columns every day linked with a different woman? And I suppose the lady in your private chamber at the Ducruet suite on my first day of duty was just an ordinary business associate. Your tax accountant, no doubt?"

"All those women were merely passing fancies, Megan. Amusements. I'm a healthy male and I'd be of no use to you if I didn't like attractive women."

Megan looked into Jacques's eyes until he avoided her gaze.

"There is safety in numbers, Meg. You like to be called Meg, don't you?"

"Nobody has ever called me that before except you."

Jacques took Megan's hand and pulled her down to sit beside him on the bed. "Meg, I love you and only you. Get that through your stubborn, beautiful head. As long as I had a string of ladies to escort here and there I was safe from any one of them—even Yolanda. Each one of those women knew she was not the only female in my life. I was always careful to make that very clear."

"You made it very clear to me too, didn't you?"

"You were different, Meg. If you'll marry me, all the rumors in the gossip columns will cease because there will be nothing left to feed them. You love me. You said you did. I suppose I can't blame you for being afraid to make yourself so vulnerable."

Jacques reached into his pocket and pulled out a diamond solitaire in a gold setting. "This ring belonged to my grandmother, Megan. I'd like for you to wear it when we announce our engagement at the gala tonight. Will you marry me?"

Megan smiled and kissed Jacques so tenderly that no verbal answer was necessary. When they parted she removed the false engagement ring from her finger and dropped it in the wastebasket.

"You've made me the happiest man in the world, Megan." Jacques reached into his pocket again. "I've also had this specially made for you."

Megan took the small square box he offered, lifted the lid and the cotton square. She gasped as she picked up a small charm in the shape of the gateway to the tin factory. It was similar to the charm her father had given her with one difference. The words on the new charm were: Taylor-Ducruet Tin.

"I can't think of a nicer gift, Jacques." Megan kissed him again. "But there's just one thing."

"What's that? Anything you want is yours. You should know that by now."

"If that is true then you'll agree that we shouldn't announce our engagement at the gala in front of strangers. I would dislike humiliating Yolanda that way and I would dislike strangers being included in such an intimate moment. Come with me."

Megan took Jacques's hand, pulling him along behind her. They left the bedroom, hurried down the stairs and across the patio.

"Jacques, do come here a moment," Yolanda called as he and Megan headed for the steps leading to the beach.

"Later, Yolanda. Later."

Megan led him through the growth of palms and seagrapes to a shaded spot about halfway between the villa and the shore. "I think it was about here, Jacques."

"What was about here?"

"I think this was the place where you kissed me that night, the night you thought I was an intruder, the night I admitted to myself that I was deeply and hopelessly in love with you." Megan held out her left hand. "Now I'm ready to accept your ring along with your love, for you have always had mine . . ."

Jacques took Megan in his arms and held her as though he would never let her go. He kissed her parted lips with the promise and passion for which she had been waiting all her life. Then he held her apart to gaze dark eyed and glowing, into her upturned face. She snuggled closer, murmuring demurely, "Shouldn't we wait until the moon is up?"

"When I am with you, the moon is always shining," said Jacques Ducruet, embracing Megan even more tightly. He had never been able to resist a beautiful woman—especially when she was the one whom he had chosen to love for the rest of his life.

Silhouette ❤ *Romance*

EXCITING MEN,
EXOTIC PLACES, HAPPY ENDINGS...

Contemporary romances for today's women

If there's room in your life for a little more romance,
SILHOUETTE ROMANCES are for you.
And you won't want to miss a single one so start
your collection now.

Each month, six very special love stories will be yours
from SILHOUETTE. Look for the
Silhouette Showcase wherever books are sold or order
now from the coupon below.

____ **#1 PAYMENT IN FULL** Anne Hampson
$1.50 (57001-3)
____ **#2 SHADOW AND SUN** Mary Carroll $1.50 (57002-1)
____ **#3 AFFAIRS OF THE HEART** Nora Powers
$1.50 (57003-X)
____ **#4 STORMY MASQUERADE** Anne Hampson
$1.50 (57004-8)
____ **#5 PATH OF DESIRE** Ellen Goforth $1.50 (57005-6)
____ **#6 GOLDEN TIDE** Sondra Stanford $1.50 (57006-4)
____ **#7 MIDSUMMER BRIDE** Mary Lewis $1.50 (57007-2)
____ **#8 CAPTIVE HEART** Patti Beckman $1.50 (57008-0)
____ **#9 WHERE MOUNTAINS WAIT** Fran Wilson
$1.50 (57009-9)

....

SILHOUETTE BOOKS, Department SB/1

1230 Avenue of the Americas, New York, N.Y. 10020

Please send me the books I have checked above. I am enclosing $_____
(please add 50¢ to cover postage and handling for each order, N.Y.S. and N.Y.C.
residents please add appropriate sales tax). Send check or money order—no
cash or C.O.D.s please. Allow up to six weeks for delivery.

NAME_____

ADDRESS_____

CITY_____ STATE/ZIP_____

SB/1-5/89